She looked at the envelope to see if there was a name on it—Beth Winston, her name, was printed neatly on the front. How strange, she thought, as she opened the envelope. There was a folded note inside. She pulled the note out, then read:

You are like a wildflower
Fragile and sweet
Admired from afar
How I wish
That I could know you better

S. W. A. K. (Sealed With A Kiss)

Other Books You Will Enjoy

A LITTLE LOVE, Virginia Hamilton
I'M NOT YOUR OTHER HALF, Caroline B. Cooney
MEGAN'S BEAT, Lou Willet Stanek
MY OWN WORST ENEMY, Margot B. McDonnell
POPULARITY PLUS, Marsha Alexander
ROADSIDE VALENTINE, C.S. Adler
WANTED: DATE FOR SATURDAY NIGHT, Janet Quin-Harkin

S.W.A.K.

Sealed With A Kiss

JUDITH ENDERLE

BERKLEY BOOKS, NEW YORK

S.W.A.K. SEALED WITH A KISS

A Berkley Book / published by arrangement with
the author

PRINTING HISTORY
Tempo edition / March 1983
Berkley edition / March 1986

ISBN: 0-425-09570-3

A BERKLEY BOOK ® TM 757,375
Berkley Books are published by The Berkley Publishing Group,
200 Madison Avenue, New York, New York 10016.
The name "BERKLEY" and the stylized "B" with design
are trademarks belonging to Berkley Publishing Corporation.

PRINTED IN THE UNITED STATES OF AMERICA

CHAPTER ONE

Cat and Mouse

Beth pushed the cart full of library books in front of her as she hummed the theme song from the musical, *Oklahoma!*

Keep your mouth shut, Beth, she told herself, stopping in the nonfiction section; otherwise the words will leak out, and you'll be singing out loud right here in the Fern Grove Public Library. Wouldn't Mrs. Forest love that! I'd be out of my part-time job and out of any more college funds.

Because she was only sixteen, Beth considered herself lucky to have a library job. The city budget had been cut, so Mrs. Forest couldn't afford another full-time librarian. But Beth had been in the right place—in the library—at the right time when Mrs. Forest had decided she would hire someone without library experience.

Beth loved the library. Working there was also handy. Fern Grove Public Library was right across the street from Meridian High where Beth went to school.

Keeping quiet was hard, however—especially today. The music in her head was driving her crazy. The songs from the school musical were mentally recorded, and she couldn't turn them off.

Mr. Jordan, the drama teacher, had played the music in class and passed out the scripts that morning. Ever since then, even when she tried to think of something else, the songs seemed to be singing inside of her—every song from the whole play.

As soon as Mr. Jordan had announced that the drama class would perform *Oklahoma!*, Beth knew which part she wanted—the female lead, the part of Laurey. Am I brave enough to try for it? she wondered as she slid three gardening books onto a shelf. I'm not afraid to sing out loud. Sometimes I even sing while I'm walking home. And I have a good voice. It's my best talent. I'm just not sure.

"Beth?"

She jumped, startled out of the *Oklahoma!* wheat fields and cornfields, where she was the lead opposite—opposite who knows? she thought. So many boys will try out. Opposite Sandy Grange, maybe. Her face warmed at the thought.

"Beth, I'm sorry to bother you," said Matt Morrow, who had pulled her out of the corn, "but I can't find a book called *Editing: The Art of Film Sculpting* by Jonathan Ross. Where should I look?"

"All the theatre books are together, Matt." She left her cart of books to show him the section.

Matt seemed to spend as much time in the library as Beth. He was a serious student. Some of the kids called him a "dexter." That was someone who had more brains than flair—kind of an out-of-it person, not one of the popular kids. Beth was sure she'd been called a "dexter" too, but never to her face. It didn't seem to bother Matt. It bothered Beth a lot.

"I've looked here," said Matt as Beth pointed to the shelves of theatre books. He was tall enough to see the top shelf straight on.

She looked for the book herself. She was sure she'd shelved it. Beth was tall also and thin, but not bony. Her skin was nice. That's what her mother said. She guessed her mother was right. She didn't get pimples.

Her friend, Ginny, said that that meant she was breaking some kind of universal law. All teenagers were supposed to get zits. It was an introduction to the suffering of real life.

But Beth felt that nice skin didn't make her pretty or popular. She suffered too—from different things. She often thought if there were tall mice, she'd fit the description of "mousy."

Beth pulled a book about Rome off a shelf. One of the books she'd shelved a few minutes before, it didn't belong on the theatre shelf. She'd made a mess of the books today. Corn in my brain, that's the problem, she thought.

"Check under Rome in the next aisle," she told Matt with a sigh.

He disappeared around the corner. Seconds later he poked his head around the shelf and held up the book. He had a nice smile and serious hazel eyes behind his dark-rimmed glasses, Beth noticed. His lashes were thick and long.

She was surprised none of the girls at school had noticed that. They were always talking about which boys had beautiful eyes. Maybe they'd never really looked at Matt. Maybe she'd noticed because she was tall also.

Beth pushed the cart to the next section and hoped she hadn't misshelved too many books during her daydreaming.

Silly to dream anyway, she thought. Even if I get a small part in the play, I'll have big problems. Play rehearsals are usually after school, and I can't be in two places at once.

But Beth didn't want to give up on trying out for a part in *Oklahoma!* If I'm chosen, I hope I can work out any conflict, she thought.

There weren't many part-time jobs for high school students in Fern Grove. The only other place a kid had a chance for a job was out at the mall, and you had to have a car or ride a very late bus if you worked there.

A West Coast tourist town in the summer, Fern Grove was dead the rest of the year, except when a film company was on location. Fern Grove was considered quaint, an East Coast setting on the Pacific. Seeing movie people so often had sparked an interest in theatre in a lot of kids—the high school drama class was always full.

Beth picked up the next book from the cart. The title was *Silent Movies*. She started back to the theatre section, the shelves she'd just left.

Study tables were at the end of the aisles. Sandy Grange, Jill Leonotti, and Elsa Nichols sat with their heads close together at one of them. Elsa and Jill were always with Sandy, like his bodyguards. What girl at Meridian High wouldn't like that job? thought

Beth, then felt the heat of a blush on her face. She wished she knew how to giggle and flirt as well as Jill and Elsa.

Suddenly the three of them laughed. Matt looked up from his table. Mrs. Forest shushed them from the front desk.

I wonder what's so funny? Beth thought.

Sandy seemed to be staring at her. He stood up.

Beth turned to the shelf, but not before she was certain that he'd winked at her. Her heart thumped in her ears. She moved the books to make room for the movie book. As she slid the volume into place, she noticed an envelope sticking out from the center pages.

People used amazing things for bookmarks: money, personal letters, utility bills, coupons, snapshots. There was a lost and found in the library, but some people never seemed to miss their bookmarks.

She looked at the envelope to see if there was a name on it—Beth Winston, her name, was neatly printed on the front. How strange, she thought, as she opened the envelope. There was a folded note inside. She pulled the note out, then read:

You are like a wildflower
Fragile and sweet
Admired from afar
How I wish
That I could know you better
S. W. A. K. (Sealed With A Kiss)

There was nothing on the back.

Who put this note here where I'd find it? she

wondered. The words were poetic, but not poetry.

Beth turned to the front cover of the book and looked inside. By reading the card, she'd know who had checked the book out last. The card in the pocket was new. That meant the old one was in small pieces somewhere. She might have typed the new card herself. Her heart fell with disappointment.

She looked down the aisle again. Sandy was writing on a paper in front of him. Jill was gone. Elsa remained at his side, slowly turning the pages of a magazine.

Sandy looked up again. He was wearing a beige Izod sweater. His eyes met Beth's. She couldn't look away. He leaned back in the chair and stretched his arms up over his head. He smiled, then ran both hands through his black curls.

He's like a cat, thought Beth, watching him—a contented cat.

She slipped the note into her jeans pocket. Could Sandy have put the envelope in the book? she wondered. Is that why he winked and smiled at me? Am I supposed to say something? Send a note in return?

"I can't," she whispered. She was the mouse again. Scurry, scurry. Hurry, hurry.

She returned to the cart, shelved the rest of the books, then went to the front counter to stamp check-outs and keep busy.

Suddenly Sandy was standing in front of her. He had a dark, even tan. His brown eyes sparkled as he looked at her. They seemed to be laughing.

Did he know I was thinking about him? Is he remembering what he wrote in the secret note? Beth felt flustered.

Elsa hung on Sandy's arm. She wore purple eyeshadow. Her pale blonde hair was short and smooth. She didn't smile. Her exotic appearance was a stark contrast to Sandy's dark good looks.

Beth wondered about his name. He wasn't "sandy" at all. Some of the teachers called him Alexander, she remembered. Why wasn't he called Alex?

She wanted to tease him. *You don't look Sandy to me. You're definitely an Alex.* That would sound dumb, Beth, silly. She didn't say anything.

Sandy put a book on the counter. Beth didn't read the title. She stamped the date due, then handed the book back to him.

"If the drama class were doing *Alice in Wonderland,* you'd make a wonderful dormouse, Beth," he said. "And I'd try out for the part of the Cheshire cat." He laughed.

For a minute Beth saw only his even, white smile and wondered if he'd read her mind earlier.

"Meow, Sandy," said Elsa, then giggled. "Let's get out of here. I'm hungry."

"See you in drama class, Beth," called Sandy, letting Elsa drag him toward the door.

"See you," Beth answered.

Through the large front library windows, she watched them go down the steps. Elsa pranced in her white boots, swinging her slender hips.

Minutes later a flash of red streaked by the library. Beth heard a low rumble. She knew that it was Sandy's sports car. Sandy Grange has everything, she thought, looks, personality, money, talent. He had had the second lead in last year's school play. A real feat for a sophomore.

"That box of new books needs pockets and cards, Beth," said Mrs. Forest, pulling Beth back to her job. She pointed to a carton of books on the floor.

"Right away, Mrs. Forest." Beth watched the head librarian flit around like a tiny sparrow, a dozen places in a single minute.

Beth went to the typewriter. Get back to work and forget about Sandy, she told herself.

But she hadn't typed even one card before she was wondering: Did Sandy slip that note into the book?

Clever phrases filled her mind. I could have said, *Cute letter, poor poetry, great sentiments* in a teasing way. I could have been bold and said, *When will we get to know each other better, Sandy?*

Even if Sandy were still here, I wouldn't say anything. I'm too shy, too afraid. She finished the card and rolled another one into the typewriter.

But curiosity wouldn't let Beth forget about the note that crinkled in her pocket whenever she moved. Did Sandy put it in the book? How could she find out?

Her best friend, Ginny, knew more about boys than she did. Ginny would know how to ask him about the note.

Before inserting another card, Beth rolled in a slip of scrap paper. She typed herself a reminder, CALL GINNY, then slipped that paper into the same pocket as the note.

CHAPTER TWO

Dreams of a "Type-A" Teenager

Beth's house was in central Fern Grove a few blocks uphill from the library. Most of the kids at Meridian lived outside of town. A few, like Sandy, lived in the beach estates. Not too many of the beach kids went to Meridian High. Most of those kids went to private schools.

Rumor said Sandy was kicked out of several private schools. Beth believed that rumors weren't always true. He could have moved to Fern Grove in the tenth grade when he first came to Meridian High.

She walked uphill toward her home thinking about the note in her pocket. The smell of rain was in the air. The wind was damp on her face. The dampness made her hair limp.

It doesn't matter, she thought, pushing a few strands back from her eyes. My hair is limp and pale anyway.

Fine was the word her mother used. But there was nothing fine about her hair that she could see. It never seemed to be long or short—always in between.

She wished she had hair like Ginny's. Her hair was thick and blue black. It billowed like great thunder clouds around her face when she walked in the wind and even when she didn't.

Once Beth told her she had a lion's mane. Ginny had laughed and said only male lions had manes and lions weren't black.

Beth's house nestled in the shelter of a circle of Monterey pines over the crest of the hill, where the street turned down again. The gray wood siding blended in with the gray day. She would have painted the house bright yellow, like the center of a daisy; but her father said that gray was less upkeep and that he had neither the time nor the money for a yellow house. He also said that it was his observation that movie people liked gray because their house was often chosen for close-up shots.

The bottom porch step creaked in the middle as Beth went up to the door. She pulled the key from her jacket pocket and pushed it into the lock. Inside, the house smelled of lemon polish and bayberry candles, her mother's favorites.

Her parents were writing a book together—something about the Indians who had once lived around Fern Grove. They'd recently begun the research and were spending hours at libraries and museums. Beth guessed she might have inherited her love of books from them.

Zorro, her cat, greeted her as she opened the door. He had sort of a Z mark on his back. Beth's mother said the name was made for him—or maybe he was made for the name. Zorro didn't seem to care what he was called as long as he was fed. He was a fat, lazy cat.

"Patience, Z." Beth leaned back against the door to close it. She hung up her jacket, then ran upstairs.

Her bedroom, like the rest of the house, had a dark oak floor. Her windows had a view into the road and farther down to the ocean. The ceiling over the windows was slanted down to a window seat piled high with a mass of pillows of various sizes and in many shades of blue.

Her cream-colored iron bed was covered with a thick patchwork quilt. On the wall over the bed hung a book-week poster that Mrs. Forest had given to Beth.

Against another wall was a special desk and chair that had come with the house. Near the closet was the cheval glass—a tilting mirror in a wood frame—that Beth's parents had given her when she'd been promoted from junior high.

A low dresser, a bedside table, a small bookshelf, plus the oval, shaggy blue bedside rug completed the furnishings.

After changing into old jeans and a green sweatshirt, Beth brushed her hair trying for an illusion of fullness that wasn't there. Giving up, she stopped in the bathroom where she washed her hands and face.

She sang a song from *Oklahoma!* In the kitchen she slipped a casserole into the oven, then fed Zorro.

Her obligations complete, Beth went into the study. The note on the telephone said her parents would be home before supper, to wait for them.

Beth dropped into her father's worn desk chair.

The bad part of living in an old house was that it seemed to set her apart from modern, suburban Fern Grove. Ginny said Beth's house seemed haunted. She didn't like to spend the night there.

"Maybe Ginny is right," mused Beth, peering into the dark corners of the study. A ghost wouldn't bother her, even if it did exist. What bothered her was the plumbing. The pipes made rude, embarrassing noises.

The study was paneled with dark wood. There were books on shelves along every wall, some piled in the corners and a few on tables.

Beth switched on the table lamp, then returned to the desk. Picking up the telephone receiver, she dialed Ginny's number.

Ginny lived in central Fern Grove too, but farther down the hill in a newer, more modern house. Her father, Mr. Rose, was president of the Fern Grove bank. She had an older sister who was married and had moved to Indiana, so Ginny was like an only child too—but nothing like Beth.

"Hi." Ginny always sounded bubbly when she answered the phone.

"Hi. It's Beth."

"I guessed. What's new? Meet anyone cute at the library today?"

"Not exactly, but something unusual did happen."

"Tell me. What?"

Beth told her about the note and Sandy.

"Oh, Sandy," she said. "He's always fooling around. The note is probably his idea of a joke. I'd forget about it, Beth."

"Sandy isn't easy to forget." Beth tried to keep her voice light.

"Beth, you aren't serious? Not about Sandy Grange!" She sounded like Beth had told her some unbelievable secret.

"What's wrong with him?" asked Beth. Ginny's sarcastic tone of voice made her angry.

I'd hoped she would help me, thought Beth. Why did I even tell her? Even though she's been dating boys since ninth grade, she doesn't know Sandy any better than I do.

"Sandy is wild," said Ginny. "You've heard the stories about him. He's bad news. Your parents would have a fit if he asked you out. You're not his type, Beth."

"Well, what type am I?" The anger sounded in her voice. She didn't want to fit into a slot stamped "Type-A" teenager. Ginny hadn't seen the note or read it. This wasn't a joke to Beth.

"You're the serious type, Beth. Sandy isn't for you," she said. "Believe me. You deserve a really nice guy."

"I never said he was for me. I don't even know for sure that he put the note in the book." Could Ginny be jealous? she wondered.

"Whoever did write that note, don't take it too seriously. There are a lot of clowns at Meridian High.

"Hey, isn't the news exciting? We're doing *Oklahoma!* this year." Ginny'd changed the subject. "Are you going to try out for the play, Beth?"

Beth relaxed and draped her legs over the arm of the chair. Zorro jumped into her lap. "I think I might try out for the part of Laurey."

She wondered, too late, if she should have shared that secret wish with Ginny. Would Ginny say that Beth wasn't the type for the lead?

"Oh, Beth, great. You'll get the lead for sure. With your voice, you can't miss."

She really is my best friend, thought Beth.

"Have you heard who's going to try out for Curly?"

"Probably a lot of the boys," said Beth quickly. Sandy was a closed subject, so she wouldn't mention him again. "What about you, Ginny? Are you going to try out for a part?"

"Me? Sing in front of all those people? Uh-uh. I'm going to sign up for scenery and props: paint giant windmills, barn doors, cornfields and wheat fields, maybe a cow or two, a real challenge to my artistic talents."

"I thought you hated art." Beth couldn't help but think about what Ginny had just said about singing in front of a lot of people. Could she do it?

"That was last semester," said Ginny. "Besides, Kevin Dennison is also signing up for scenery and props."

"Should have guessed. Hasn't he succumbed to your charm yet?"

"He will. He will. I'll paint him right into a corner if I have to."

The front door clicked open, then banged shut. A cold draft encircled Beth.

"Dinner smells good, Beth," her mother called.

"I have to hang up, Ginny. See you in school tomorrow."

"All right. Bye."

Beth's mother poked her head into the study, waking Zorro from his catnap on Beth's lap. "It's raining," she said. "I'll set the table. Will you make some biscuits?"

"Sure, Mom." Beth stretched like Zorro.

Her mother seemed to have endless energy. She floated from task to task and was very efficient, a perfect complement to Beth's father, who usually buried himself in his work and only surfaced for necessities like eating and sleeping. Sometimes Beth thought he was startled to see her, as if he'd forgotten he had a daughter. Her mother assured her she was wrong about this.

As she left the study, her father came slowly down the stairs. "We made great progress today, didn't we, Myra?" he called to Beth's mother. No comment nor answer was expected to his statement. His head was down, his glasses balanced on the end of his nose. He was reading a notebook as he walked and seemed not to notice that Beth was in the hallway. She loved him despite his apparent one-trackedness.

The kitchen was large with an old double-oven stove. A round oak table was centered in the room. Dinner smelled good. Beth's stomach growled.

Her mother hummed to herself as she placed silverware on top of yellow napkins next to ironstone plates.

"How was school?" she asked. Silver strands threaded through her pale hair, which she tied back with blue yarn. Her face was young and calm. She looked at Beth and waited for an answer.

"Fine. Mr. Jordan said there'd be tryouts for this year's play right after mid-semester grades. We'll be doing *Oklahoma!*"

"Will you try out?"

"Uh-huh." Beth set the blue mixing bowl on the counter and took the flour canister from the shelf.

"Good. I hope you get the part you want, honey."

"I think I'm going to try out for the lead, Mom." She'd told two people. If she told one more, she'd have to do it.

"The lead?" Her mother looked surprised, but she smiled. "Good, Beth. We'll be proud even if you get only a small part. But you might just get the lead if a senior doesn't have priority. I'm glad you're trying." Her mother came and put her arm around Beth and hugged her. They were almost the same height.

"My job might be a problem."

Flour, salt, baking powder—Beth measured the biscuit ingredients into the bowl and mixed while she talked.

"If you get the part, I'm sure Mrs. Forest and Mr. Jordan will help you arrange a schedule for both."

"Do you think so?" Hope rose inside her as she rolled the dough lightly, then cut round circles with a floured glass.

"Yes, I think so."

Beth tried not to think of the seniors in the drama class. Would Mr. Jordan be partial to them? He never had been before. But the Meridian High drama class had never performed such a big production before either.

Her mother sounded so confident, Beth believed

she had a chance. The lead in *Oklahoma!* could be hers.

The oven was ready for the biscuits. Waiting for them to bake, Beth's thoughts turned to Sandy. She hadn't told her mother about the note. That wasn't the kind of thing she could discuss with her.

The biscuits almost burned while she day-dreamed. Her mother believed she was thinking of the play. She would have been surprised if she'd known Beth was dreaming about the probable male lead.

Outside, the night was black, and rain tapped at the row of square windowpanes.

Her mother smiled as she put the steaming casserole in the center of the table and left to tell Beth's father that dinner was ready.

Beth finished putting the food on the table and sat down at her place.

What would it be like to be kissed by Sandy Grange? she wondered, while her mother said grace.

After dinner Beth went up to her room. She didn't open her books right away. She sat at the old oak desk, the one that came with the house. There was a secret compartment under the center drawer. Beth kept valentines, special letters from her grandmother, and her diary in it. She pulled the drawer out and set it on top of the desk. She slid a board forward to expose the shallow, gift-box sized space. Going to the closet, she took the note from the pocket of her jeans, then added it to the other precious papers in the desk. From the space she took out her diary.

There were quite a few blank pages for days when

nothing had happened at all. She opened to that day's page.

Dear Diary,

As usual I worked in the library after school. Something exciting happened. I was putting a book about silent movies on the shelf when I noticed an envelope sticking from between the pages. I opened it and. . .

The entry she wrote that night was the longest ever.

Maybe every page will have a long entry, she thought, now that I have a secret admirer. I hope he doesn't remain secretive for long though—especially since I think I know who he is.

Sandy's Cheshire-cat smile and laughing eyes took form clearly in her mind.

CHAPTER THREE

The Third Person

Waking up to the sound of rain and the aroma of freshly perked coffee felt cozy. Beth wanted to stay in bed, listen to the pitter-patter of drops on the roof, and watch the tiny rivers trickle down the windowpanes. Hurry, lazy bones, she told herself throwing the covers back. You'll be late for school.

Blue corduroy pants and a bulky white fisherman's sweater were perfect rainy weather clothes. She tied her hair back with a piece of her mother's blue yarn, then hurried downstairs.

From the study came the sound of two typewriters—her parents already hard at work.

A glass of milk and two warmed-over biscuits spread with butter and plum jam were her breakfast. She knew she should eat more, but that morning she had no appetite.

Don't think about the note or Sandy, Beth told herself, as she thought of nothing else—except perhaps the play.

"I'm leaving for school now," she called into the study.

Both of her parents looked up for a second when she opened the door, but they kept on typing.

"Wear your raincoat and boots," said her mother. Her fingers pounded staccato letters on white paper. "We might go over to Pebble Rock Museum if the weather eases. If we're late tonight, don't wait dinner. Eat without us."

"All right."

Beth's navy blue raincoat lost a button as she slipped it on. Fortunately the belt covered the spot. The boots she wore weren't the ones her mother meant, but they were boots. Her Christmas present, they were dark brown leather that hugged her legs. No one wore clunky rubber boots to school at Meridian, even if it did look like the start of the second Great Flood outside.

She lifted her umbrella from the old milk can by the door and stepped out onto the porch. Water ran in long streams off the eaves. She turned up her collar, popped the umbrella, then ventured out into the downpour.

Ginny would be riding to school with her father. As Beth started down the hill toward school, she watched for their white Cadillac. But Ginny was already at their locker when Beth arrived.

"I asked Daddy to stop by your house, but he said it was too early," she told Beth.

"He was right. I was sleepy this morning." Beth shook her umbrella before putting it in the bottom of the locker, then hung her coat on a hook.

Ginny was putting on light-colored lipstick while

looking in the tiny mirror stuck inside the locker door.

"Hello, Beth." Matt Morrow loomed tall beside the lockers. He was wearing dark brown corduroy pants and a brown V-neck sweater over a green and beige plaid shirt. His glasses were slightly steamed. He took them off and rubbed them on his sleeve. How different he looked without them! The thought that he fit the description "sandy" flashed through Beth's mind.

"I was wondering if you'd thought about trying out for the lead in the school play this year?" he asked.

How did he know? wondered Beth. Did Ginny tell him? I know her. She's watching us in the little mirror while pretending to fix her hair. She's been arranging that same curl since Matt arrived.

"Um, I might try out for the lead," she said hesitantly. Had she told three people now?

"I hope you do. When Mr. Jordan announced that we'd be doing *Oklahoma!*, I thought of you," said Matt. "You're perfect for the part of Laurey."

"Thanks." Beth had forgotten he was in her drama class.

"Oh, and I appreciated your help yesterday at the library."

"That's part of my job."

He shifted his books and looked at her as if he wanted to say more. "Well, I'll see you," he said, then was gone.

"He's shy. Kind of cute, too. I've seen him before but can't place him. Who is he?" Ginny's eyes glowed with curiosity.

"Oh, that's Matt Morrow. He's at the library all the time. Guess he's a real brain, from what I hear. He does have nice eyes."

Ginny smiled and nodded. "Is he in any of your classes?"

"Just drama. He's a senior."

"Of course! Drama! That's where I've seen him. He sits way in back. And he's a senior?" Ginny seemed impressed. "Has he ever asked you out?"

"Matt? I don't think he's ever asked anyone out. He rarely ever talks to me."

"He talked to you today." Ginny's voice was teasing.

"That's just because I helped him find a book yesterday. Don't make a big deal out of nothing, Ginny."

"If you say so," she said. "Have you got all your books from the locker?"

Beth grabbed her physics book, then Ginny slammed the locker door.

"See you in drama." She blended into the passing throng.

Down the hall Beth saw Sandy. He wore a black and red jacket shiny from the rain. His hair was wet too, and it hung in curly strands around his face and part way into his eyes. He was coming toward her.

Why did I let Ginny close the locker? wondered Beth. I don't have time to spin the combination. My hair is probably a mess. I haven't looked in a mirror since I arrived at school.

She didn't want to be caught staring, but her feet seemed stuck. Quickly she leaned against the locker door and pretended to search her notebook for a nonexistent paper.

The group with Sandy laughed and talked loudly.

Glancing up as they passed, Beth hoped he'd see her. *Hi, Beth, he'd say. Oh, hi, Sandy,* she'd answer as if they talked all the time. But he had already passed. Watching his back as he swept down the hall, she noticed that his arm was around Pamela Casey. The top of Pam's head barely reached his shoulder. She was never part of his group before. What had she done to make him notice her? Beth sighed, trying not to feel too much disappointment at his lack of recognition. He would have said hello if he'd seen me, she reassured herself. His feelings for me are special. He's shy because he's more serious about me. I'm not like the other girls he flirts and teases with.

He isn't your type. She remembered Ginny's words. He is. I want him to be. I want to be his type. I'm tired of being a mouse, she thought. Sandy and Beth. Our names even sound good together. He'll wait until he has a minute alone, I'm sure. Then he'll ask, *Did you get my note?* He'll look serious, anxious to know how I feel. Beth had never felt that way about any boy.

The bell rang, startling her back to the present. She had to hurry. Physics class was upstairs. She had only a few minutes to get there on time.

It had been a long, slow day. Beth sat in Latin class and drew wreaths of flowers—wildflowers?—across the top of her paper.

The day's lessons were a blur. Only drama class stood out. Remembering that made her sit up and pay attention to Mr. Slater.

"All grades count in this class," Mr. Jordan had told them that day in drama. "The end of March is mid-semester. If, by then, you don't have a C or better in every class you're taking, you won't be eligible to try out for any of the major roles in *Oklahoma!* I know this sounds tough, but *Oklahoma!* is going to be a time-consuming production. We'll have to push to be ready for our June performance. Since I don't want to take time away from your other classes, if you're behind at mids, you must realize you won't have the time to give to extensive rehearsals. Choose your desired role accordingly."

There had been a lot of groans and that's-not-fairs from the class.

"You have time to bring your grades up," Mr. Jordan had said.

Beth's grades weren't a problem. Most classes were fairly easy for her, though she did have to put in study time each night—especially in math. Advanced algebra was much more difficult than she'd expected, and neither of her parents could help her with it. Fortunately, Ginny's father was a math whiz, and Ginny could usually explain a problem that had stumped Beth. At present she had a B average.

Mr. Slater said they had to memorize a Latin poem for homework. That won't be difficult, thought Beth, making a note of the assignment in her folder. If I can put the words to music, I'll remember them easily.

The final bell rang. School was over for the day. The halls were chaos as locker doors slammed and everyone rushed for the exits.

Beth and Ginny were part of the mass evacuation. The rain hadn't let up at all, but that didn't slow anyone down.

"I'm going to call my dad and ask him to pick me up at the library," said Ginny as they dodged puddles on the school's front walk. "I'll study there until five-thirty."

They waited on the curb for traffic to clear. A familiar red sports car roared past, sending a shower of muddy water toward them. They jumped back just in time, getting only a few brown splatters.

The top of the car was down. Beth heard the laughter of those packed into the small seats. She pretended she didn't know who was driving.

Ginny said nothing, but her look said a lot.

They crossed the street and ran up the library steps.

"Mr. Jordan sure made it easier for you today," said Ginny.

"What do you mean?" Beth shook the rain off her umbrella, then followed her friend inside.

"How many girls will be trying out for the lead now, with the grade restrictions?"

"A lot," said Beth.

"Name five."

"Bonnie Raymond, Kate Harte, Joan Kaminski, Mary Sue Green."

"That's only four."

"Me?" Beth's voice sounded as little as the word.

"You don't have any competition," said Ginny.

Beth wanted to believe her. I can't back out now, she thought. My decision has been made. I'm relieved and scared. What if I don't get the part? What if I do?

The library was quiet that day. The rain had sent everyone hurrying for the coziness of home. Even Matt Morrow's regular table was empty.

Ginny put her books down and went to use the pay phone.

Beth hung her raincoat in the office and went in search of Mrs. Forest. I hope she has a lot of work for me to do today, she thought. Thinking about the play, everyone and everything connected with it, made her feel very confused.

CHAPTER FOUR

Hope Renewed

Dear Diary,

I'm beginning to believe Ginny is right. Sandy comes to the library all the time. He's still a big tease, but he hasn't mentioned the note—not even hinted about it. I still have the note. Maybe he'll never admit he put it in that book. I try not to think of that. Why wouldn't he want me to know he wrote it?

I've memorized a lot of the lines from *Oklahoma!* Now I'd better get some homework done, or I won't qualify for the lead at all.

Love,

B. W.

Beth opened her books after putting her diary away, but she couldn't concentrate. She'd had that problem a lot lately. She was afraid she'd flunked the math test that day, too. She promised herself she'd do extra studying over the weekend.

The night before she'd meant to study but got

caught up writing in her diary and practicing more lines. Everyone in class was learning all the parts. Mr. Jordan said that that way anyone could be an understudy for anyone else.

"I won't go to sleep until I do ten math problems," Beth said. She yawned and started on the first.

Another day almost gone. Beth finished the children's books then moved to the adult section.

She hadn't flunked her algebra test the day before. She'd gotten a D, which was as bad. Now she had to work twice as hard to keep her average up, at least until mid-semester. Between math, the play, and wondering about Sandy, her head was in a constant whirl. She felt like three different people: Beth, the student; Beth, the actress; and Beth. . .

"Hello, Beth. Penny for your thoughts."

She jumped, dropping the library books she was supposed to be putting away. As she bent down to pick them up, Sandy bent also, and they banged heads.

"I'm sorry." Beth wished she could crawl under the tweed carpet. Her face was crimson, she knew. Together they managed to pick up three books. How ridiculous she felt.

"Come and talk with me for a minute." Sandy placed one book in her hand.

Beth had grabbed the other two and held them awkwardly against her. "About what?" The words were almost stammered out.

"Let's sit down," he said.

She put the books on the cart, then followed him to a vacant study table.

Sandy dropped down in one chair. Beth took the one opposite. Today his eyes weren't sparkling. His face was serious. Is he going to tell me about the note? she wondered. She watched him intently.

"You know how sticky old Jordan is about grades," he said. "All those stupid rules about C's or no part in the play."

"No major part." Beth nodded her head.

"Only one part interests me," said Sandy. "I want to be Curly."

"How about Will or Jud?" Beth didn't know why she asked the question. Sandy wanted what she wanted.

"I said Curly," said Sandy firmly. He tipped the chair back on two legs.

What if he falls over? wondered Beth. What will I do? She was supposed to be working, not talking. She watched him balance and silently hoped he was good at it, so Mrs. Forest wouldn't notice that she wasn't shelving books.

"Anyway, I'm managing C's in most of my classes. The only one I'm really messing up in is math. If I don't do better, I'll flunk. Then, not only will I miss out on the play, but also my old man will disown me. *So* . . . ," he emphasized the word and let the chair drop back onto all four legs again. His dark eyes stared into Beth's as he leaned forward. His hand was only inches away from hers on the table. "*So*," he said again, "I want you to help me with my math, Beth. Fellow actors and actresses stick together. They give aid and assistance in time of need. Right?" His dark eyes pleaded.

He reminded Beth of a cocker spaniel puppy she'd seen in a pet store when she was little. How badly she'd wanted him to be hers.

"Beth? Say you'll help me."

"Sandy, I'd like to." Her mind scrambled for the right words to explain. "I can't. Math is my toughest class this year too. I pulled a D on this last test."

"The first D this year, I bet. It'll be easy for you to help me, Beth. You're right here every day. We can meet after school." He reached across and put his hand over hers. She took a deep breath and was afraid to move. His skin was warm against hers. "Come on. Don't say no." He smiled.

Beth swallowed. "It's not that I don't want to help, Sandy," she said. "But this is my job. I can't risk losing it. I don't even take time out to do my own homework. I shouldn't be sitting here with you now."

Sandy pulled his hand back. Beth stood up and looked toward the front counter. Mrs. Forest was busy typing.

Sandy's smile faded as she looked back at him. He sighed loudly. "I thought I could count on you, Beth," he said, running one hand through his dark curls. "It'll be on your conscience if I'm not in the play."

She stood by the table, holding the back of the chair, reluctant to leave yet unable to say yes to his request.

He stood up slowly.

"Believe me, I'd like to help, Sandy, if I knew the math any better myself, or if I could take the time from my work." A feeling of excitement passed through her. "I know. How about a different time? At lunch or—"

"I've got a busy schedule too," said Sandy. "After school is the time I want to study. Say you'll help me, Beth. Find a way," he demanded. "I got an F on the test."

Beth sighed. "I can't." The words sounded louder than she intended. Several people looked in her direction. Quickly she turned to go back to work, certain she'd ruined any possible chance she might have had with Sandy.

She noticed Matt studying at a nearby table. The sight of him made Beth turn back to Sandy. "I've got an idea," she said.

His eyes brightened. "You'll do it."

"No." Beth shook her head. "But the boy over at that table is Matt Morrow. I'll introduce you. He's really smart, Sandy. Maybe he would help you."

A strange smile turned up one corner of Sandy's mouth. "Nah," he said. "Forget it. I know Morrow, and I couldn't study with him. He'd make me feel stupid. I really wanted *your* help, Beth." He stepped back suddenly and almost knocked the chair over. Quickly he caught it and shoved it noisily into place against the table.

Beth winced.

"Must be nice to be a brain. Guess you and Morrow have a corner on the smarts around here. Well, I'll see you around. You'd better get back to work."

"But I'm not sma . . ." Beth watched him take long, quick steps down the fiction aisle. Finally she started back toward the cart. From someplace near the front desk, she heard Elsa's giggle. Several people looked up from their reading again.

There was a tightness in Beth's throat as she carried a book to the end of the aisle to get what might be her last close glimpse of Sandy. He, Elsa, Jill, and Pam strode, arms locked, toward the library door. When they couldn't all exit at once, they burst into laughter.

Mrs. Forest got up from her desk chair. "Please," she said in a hushed voice.

Sandy stepped to one side. He bowed low to Mrs. Forest and then to the girls. The girls passed him, heads in the air. Beth heard another burst of laughter before the door closed behind them.

I should have said yes, she thought. Maybe if I hurried with my library jobs, I could help him. I could tell him that Mrs. Forest gave me permission. She sighed out loud as she pushed the book cart over to nonfiction. She knew she was kidding herself. Her work rarely got completed; there was always something left for the next time. Mrs. Forest would say that she would have to make a choice, her job or tutoring Sandy, and she'd already chosen.

Through blurred eyes, she read the title of the next book. Her throat ached. Beth coughed to keep the tears from making rivers on her cheeks. In her hand she held the book on silent movies, the one where she'd found the mystery note. She noticed that the *i* in movies had faded so that the title seemed to say *Silent Moves*. As Beth lifted the book toward the shelf, she saw the corner of an envelope. With trembling hands she pulled it from between the pages.

Like the previous note, her name was centered on the envelope in neat, printed letters. Quickly she opened the flap and took out the folded paper. After a quick look around, she unfolded the note and read:

Dear Beth,

One day soon we will get better acquainted.

S. W. A. K. (Sealed With A Kiss)

Beth read the note twice before refolding it and slipping it into her skirt pocket. This message wasn't an attempt at poetry, but the message made her tears recede and hope rise in their place.

Sandy must have slipped the envelope into the book before he spoke to me, thought Beth. But will he still mean what he wrote now that I can't help him? She pushed that thought away. There must be some way I can help him with his algebra. Maybe if I asked Matt for him. . .

Beth started toward the study table where Matt always sat before she realized that he was gone. Would he help Sandy? she wondered.

Then she remembered the book card. This time she'd see Sandy's name written there. She would know for sure that he wrote the note. Beth opened the cover of the book. The card was gone; the pocket was empty. She put the book on the bottom of the cart. "I'll have to type a new card," she said disappointedly. "Why is Sandy being so mysterious?"

As quickly as possible, Beth shelved the rest of the library books. It was almost time for her to go home. She had a lot to think about that weekend. She slipped her hand inside her skirt pocket to touch the second note.

CHAPTER FIVE

Cloud Ninety-Nine

The hill seemed steeper that day, maybe because her mind and heart were distracted, and she wasn't enjoying the walk home. Beth passed familiar Victorian frame houses, some with white picket fences. Early spring flowers bloomed in a few of the front yards. Their cheerful colors failed to lift her feelings of gloom.

Near the crest of the hill, she looked down to the ocean. White caps dotted the surface of the water. A mist hung on the horizon, pinkish from the late afternoon sun. Spring was everywhere. Spring—"when a young man's fancy lightly turns to thoughts of love." The Tennyson line came unbidden into her mind. Beth remembered the note in her pocket. Someone's thoughts were turned in that direction.

As she started to walk again, she heard the roar of a motor behind her. A familiar red sports car screeched to a stop at the curb beside her.

"Hey, Beth. How about a ride home?" Sandy's dark curls were blown wild from the ride. His face was ruddy. He didn't look angry or upset.

"I live only a couple houses farther." Beth wished it weren't true.

"Then, how about going out with me tomorrow night? We'll go to the show. You can't turn me down three times in one day." He grinned, and Beth's heart melted.

Ginny's words flashed into her mind. How she wished she hadn't mentioned Sandy to her friend. Beth hesitated. Should she ask her parents first?

"Can't wait for an answer, if you aren't sure." Sandy gunned the motor. The car rolled back slightly.

"It's not that—" began Beth hurriedly.

"What's your phone number? I'm late getting home. I'll call you tonight," he said.

"Five, five, five, eight, four, three, four." The numbers rattled out.

"Eight, four, three, four." he repeated.

Beth hoped he wouldn't forget. Before she could offer to write them down, he was gone, a flash of red swinging a turn in the street, then a roar down the hill.

Typewriters were clacking away when Beth opened the front door. Their clackety-clack clashed with the tick-tock of the grandfather clock at the end of the hall.

Zorro jumped from a chair in the living room and came to remind Beth that he was hungry. She picked him up and held him close, much to his displeasure. "Sandy's going to call me, Z." In the middle of the entry hall, she whirled around with the cat in her arms before turning him loose again.

Even saying my dream-come-true out loud doesn't make it believable, she thought. The phone will have to ring before I'll know I'm not dreaming and that I really have been asked out by Sandy.

She went back and nudged the front door with her hip. It slammed shut, but the typing didn't stop.

Zorro meowed loudly again to express his opinion, then returned to his chair. Beth raced up the stairs two at a time. After I change I'll call Ginny, she thought. Won't she be surprised!

Flopping onto her bed, her happiness exploded in song. Staring up at the ceiling, with all its familiar spots and lines, Beth sang a medley from *Oklahoma!* The music seemed to charge her feet. On the final note, she jumped up. Holding a small, white, lace-trimmed pillow from her bed, she hummed the songs through again and danced in circles around her room. She felt as if she were in a movie.

Breathless, she dropped onto the blue cushions on the windowseat. She gazed out to the ocean. The sun burned a red line around the edge of the haze as it slid down toward the horizon. "I can't wait," she whispered and hugged herself.

"Beth, is that you? Come downstairs and tell me about your day."

"All right, Mom. Be down in a minute."

Quickly she changed from her school clothes into old jeans and a blue print blouse. She twirled out the door and skipped down the stairs. Beth reached the bottom landing without ever having consciously touched one step.

Her mother was waiting for her. "You look happy," she said. "Have you tried out for the part in the play?"

"Play? Part? Oh, not yet. Soon, Mom."

"You passed a difficult test?"

Beth wanted to laugh. No part of school had ever made her feel like doing cartwheels and singing at the same time. "I'm expecting a call. Sandy Grange, a boy from school, asked me to the show tomorrow night. He's going to call to find out if I can go. It is all right, isn't it?"

"A boy asked you to the show?" Her father came from the study.

Surprised that he'd heard her, Beth felt her mouth drop open.

"Yes, a boy. Your little girl is growing up." Her mother put her hand on Beth's shoulder and gave a quick squeeze.

"Who is this boy? Where does he live? Where are you going? What time?" It seemed as if a thousand questions flew from her father's lips.

Beth tried to answer him calmly. "Sandy goes to school with me. He lives on the beach. I don't know what time, but there's only one movie theatre the kids go to, the one out at the mall. The one in town shows only old movies."

"It would be better if you went out with a group," said her father.

"Mom, it's just the show—" began Beth.

"David, I'm sure this will be all right. Beth knows this boy."

"Home by eleven," said her father abruptly and retreated to the study.

"What if the movie isn't over by then, Mom?" Beth was stunned by the intense attention from her father.

"It should be, honey. Check the newspaper or call

so we know the time. This is your first date, after all. Your father and I don't adjust as easily as you do to your growing up." She smoothed Beth's hair with her hand, then swatted her behind as if she were still a little kid. "Now take care of Zorro. He's been complaining the past half hour. And please stir the spaghetti sauce. I have to help your father outline chapter three." She followed after him into the study.

Hurriedly Beth fed Zorro, then stirred the sauce. She lifted the spoon, inhaled, blew on it, then took a little taste. "Mmmm. Good." She felt hungry but didn't think she'd be able to eat much. With all the excitement inside, there wouldn't be room for spaghetti.

Finally she lifted the receiver from the kitchen phone and dialed Ginny's number.

"Ginny? It's me, Beth."

"Your voice sounds funny. What's wrong?" asked Ginny.

"Wrong? Nothing." Suddenly Beth decided not to tell her about Sandy. What if he forgot to call? Ginny would say, I told you so.

"I called to ask about algebra homework," she said quickly. "What pages do we have Monday? I want to get it out of the way."

"No pages and all the pages. We have a test. Don't tell me you forgot. That's not like you, Beth."

"Is it *this* Monday?" Beth pretended she didn't know.

"Yes. Where were you during class? Daydreaming about Matt Morrow, I bet."

"Matt! You're kidding. He's too busy studying to pay attention to anyone."

"Boy, are you blind. He spends most of drama class watching you."

"Boy, are you seeing things."

"You'd see too, if you'd look," said Ginny.

"Listen, I have to stir the spaghetti sauce. Thanks for reminding me about the test."

"You're welcome. See you Monday." Ginny hung up.

"Matt Morrow!" Beth hung up the phone and shook her head. "What a crazy idea!"

Dinner was over. Beth's parents had gone back to their writing. She was left to do the dishes. She rattled the pot in the sink as she scrubbed the spaghetti sauce from the sides. The activity helped cool her temper.

All during dinner her father had quizzed and lectured her about dating. He'd spoken more that night than in the whole past month. She wished he'd remained quiet and stayed lost in his Indian book. Beth sloshed water in the pot. Her mother had tried to soften his orders, but she wasn't very effective. Beth had felt like she was five again and asking to play in front instead of in the tiny backyard. Why was one movie such a big deal? She'd even called to check the movie time. That still hadn't seemed to satisfy her father.

The phone rang. Beth dropped the pot with a clatter, then raced to answer it.

"Is this Beth?" Sandy's voice sounded deeper on the phone.

"Yes." She struggled to catch her breath and keep her heart from banging too loudly.

"Well?"

"I'd love to go to the show tomorrow night."

"Good. I'll be by at eight. Listen for the car."

The phone hummed. He'd hung up. I guess boys don't talk like girls do, thought Beth, replacing the receiver. She felt let down after waiting all that time for his call. Stay calm, she thought. He only needed a yes or no. What more was there to say?

She returned to the sink and began to scrub the pot again, this time in slow motion. What would she wear? She was certain she had nothing right for going to the show with Sandy.

Her father's list of rules and regulations were pushed to the back of her mind. She wouldn't worry about them. Surely Sandy would understand if she had to come right home.

As Beth dreamed of the next night, she dumped half a pot of soapy water down the front of her and all over the floor. It didn't matter. She reached for a rag. Cloud nine was miles below. She was on cloud ninety-nine. Sandy Grange wanted to take Beth Winston to the show the next night. She couldn't wait.

CHAPTER SIX

The Show

Nothing to wear! I knew it, thought Beth. My pants are all old. My skirts don't match my sweaters. My dresses are too dressy. Nothing I own is right for going to the show tonight.

She pulled her brown corduroy pants off the hanger again. Maybe—with her white sweater—they weren't too bad. But they didn't look special enough. She should have gone shopping, but her mother said that until the advance came on their book, money was tight, and Beth hated to dip into her college fund.

In her top drawer she found a small cat pin with golden eyes. She pinned it near the neck of her sweater. It helped a little.

Now her hair, hopeless as always. She'd tried curling it and had to wash it again, it had looked so weird. "Now I know why my mother has had those curlers stored in the bottom of the linen closet forever," she muttered as she pulled the brush through her fine, straight hair. "They don't work."

She made a face at herself in the mirror. "At least my hair shines."

Ginny and Beth had done a lot of experimenting with makeup, so she knew that a little blusher and mascara did wonders for her. A touch of blue eye shadow to match her eyes, some lipgloss, and a squirt of violet cologne, then she was ready.

And not a minute too soon. She heard the sound of Sandy's car. She clattered down the stairs in record time. The bell would ring any minute. Beth took her jacket from the closet and smoothed her hair to be sure it was all right.

She heard the impatient sound of the horn again. Looking at the clock she saw that it was ten past eight. I guess Sandy thinks we'll be late if he comes in, she thought. He can meet my parents later. I know they'll wait up.

With her jacket on and her purse in her hand, she ran to the study. "I'm going," she called, then turned and hurried out of the front door before her parents could push away from their typewriters or answer.

Beth stepped off the bottom step as Sandy gave the horn another blast.

"Hi, Sandy," she said as she opened the car door.

"Hi. Hurry up." He put the gas pedal to the floor almost before she had the car door closed.

Beth was thrust back in the seat and grabbed onto the door handle. The wind made quick destruction of her smooth hair. The roar of the motor and squeal of tires echoed behind them. She refused to think what her father would say.

Sandy reached over and patted her leg.

She jumped.

"Hey, relax, Beth," he said. "I've been driving since I was fourteen. No one can handle this sweetheart like I can."

"Fourteen! But I thought—I had to wait until I was sixteen to get my license." She'd only been driving since the past summer and didn't really have a chance to drive much. The Winstons had only one car, and it wasn't always running. "How did you get your license so young?"

Sandy laughed. "You're cute, Beth," he said.

She felt dumb as she realized he hadn't had a license when he was fourteen either. He drove anyway.

The show parking lot was crowded. There was a long line waiting to get in. The picture showing was called *Love Forever Young*. It was supposed to be good.

As they pulled into the lot, Sandy pounded out a salute on the car horn to everyone there. He waved as they passed the line, then turned sharply into a small parking space. He didn't open his car door, just climbed out over the side like a character in a television show.

"Come on, Beth. Let's see who else is here," he called.

Beth opened her door, trying not to bump the car next to her, and squeezed out.

Sandy grabbed her hand, and they ran across the parking lot.

"Hey, Sandy, new girl?" someone called.

"He manufactures them," answered someone else.

Sandy waved and called teasing remarks in return

as they hurried toward the end of the line.

Beth's face tingled from the cool night air. She felt excited, special, being with him. She could feel herself smiling.

"Stay here," he said as they reached the end of the line. "There are a couple people I have to see." He was gone before she could answer.

Beth looked up the long string of waiting people and saw him moving from spot to spot, always smiling, sometimes laughing. I wish I were with him, she thought.

"Hi, Beth. Are you here alone?"

She turned around, surprised to hear her name. Matt was standing behind her. She hadn't heard him come up. "Oh, hi, Matt," she said. "I came with Sandy. He's up there talking to someone. He seems to know half the people in this line."

Matt smiled and jammed his hands in his jacket pockets. "I've heard this movie is really great. Remember when they were filming?"

"Yes. I heard it turned out well too. I wonder if my house will be in it?"

"What color is your house?"

"Gray with pine trees down both sides."

"I'll watch for it," said Matt.

The line started to move quickly. Beth was almost to the ticket window. Where was Sandy? For a second she felt panicky.

"Hey, I turn my back for a minute, and you're getting picked up by some other guy." Sandy slipped into line behind her and put both arms around her waist. He pulled her close. She could feel his breath on her face. His dark hair brushed her cheek. She was surprised and didn't know whether to feel embarrassed or hope that everyone noticed. Sandy let go of her and turned to Matt. "Don't be trying to steal my girl, Morrow," he said.

Matt didn't answer Sandy.

They were up to the window now. Sandy bought two tickets.

"I'll see you in school, Beth," said Matt as Sandy and Beth walked toward the theatre entrance. She nodded and waved.

They sat on the right side of the theatre, more than halfway down the aisle. The movie was sad and beautiful. Some of it was funny too, but it wasn't a comedy. It was about two older people, like grandparents, who met in a park and fell in love.

It's nice that older people still have feelings for each other, thought Beth. Her house wasn't in the picture, but there was some familiar scenery.

She couldn't concentrate on the movie. Sandy kept his arm around her. A couple of times he kissed her ear. She liked it but felt embarrassed.

"Could we have some popcorn?" she whispered.

"Sure." Sandy left at the most interesting part of the movie. He returned with a large container of buttered popcorn. Beth didn't have to worry about eating it all, though, because he threw half of it at the people in front of them. Torn between telling him to stop and laughing at him, she didn't do anything. He's crazy, she thought. If we go to a show again, I'll ask to see a comedy.

Go again! I wonder if he'll ask again, she wondered. He did say I was his girl, didn't he? Did he mean it? How can he know so quickly? He doesn't even know me yet.

The movie was over at ten minutes before eleven.

"Want to go to The Wharf?" asked Sandy. That was the local burger place. All the kids went there after dates. Beth had only been there a couple of times when some of the girls went in a group.

"Not tonight," said Beth as they walked toward the car.

"Me, neither," said Sandy. He backed the car out and zoomed out of the driveway. "I know a wonderful deserted beach," he said.

"No, I—I have to be home early." Beth wished she could go to The Wharf. Saying that she had to go home sounded like an excuse. She couldn't say that she wouldn't know what to do on a deserted beach, and she was afraid to say that she didn't want to find out. She wanted Sandy to like her.

"Sure," he said, shifting the car through its gears.

"I'm sorry. My father—"

"Hey, don't worry. My folks get on my case all the time too. Sometimes you can't get past them."

He stopped the car in front of Beth's house at eleven-fifteen.

"Thank you for the show, Sandy," she said.

He leaned over and gave her a quick kiss on the lips, so fast she was hardly aware it happened.

"I love a challenge. How about next weekend? Sunday? We'll go ice skating at The New Igloo, the rink that opened on the other side of the mall. Can you tell me now?" His eyes sparkled in the light from the street lamp.

Why will skating be a challenge? wondered Beth. Maybe he didn't know how. But that wouldn't matter. She wasn't that great a skater herself. It had been a long time since she'd been on the ice.

"Well?"

"Yes, I'd love to go," she said. I'll tell my parents I'm going, she thought. After all I'm old enough to make my own decisions.

Sandy reached across her and opened the car door. "See you Monday."

"You can come in." Beth slid out of the car. "I could make hot chocolate."

"Not tonight."

Minutes later the car was swallowed up in the night. Only the roar of the motor seemed to remain behind.

Beth's head spun. She felt as if she'd been on a merry-go-round and was still turning. She touched her lips, trying to remember the brief good night kiss. He must like her. He'd asked her out again and kissed her.

It was so hard to know if you were doing the right things, saying the right words, with someone like Sandy. Other girls seemed to know. Ginny knew. She was popular.

"I guess I'm doing all right," said Beth as she went slowly up the walk.

She let herself in. A light shone from the study. Quietly she walked to the door and looked in. Her father was going over his notes. Her mother sat on the old couch, her feet up. She was reading.

"I'm home," said Beth.

"Did you have fun?" asked her mother. "Was the movie good?"

Beth nodded. "Our house wasn't in it," she said.

"Is the young man with you?" asked her father without looking up.

"No. He had to go," said Beth.

"Come in and sit down," said her father.

"I'm tired," she said. "I'll tell you more about the show in the morning, OK? Good night." Beth turned and ran up the stairs. Her bedroom door closed with a bang. Her parents wouldn't come after her, she knew. For once she was glad her father was busy. She didn't want to answer a lot of questions, and she could guess the kind her father might ask.

When I see Sandy at school, I'll tell him they were disappointed they didn't meet him, she thought. Next time he'll come in. She pulled off her sweater and folded it. Maybe he was afraid. Maybe, like with the notes, he was too shy. That's it, she told herself. All his clowning around and craziness is a cover-up for shyness. Didn't I read a book with a character like that recently? I'm sure I did, but I can't remember the title.

She hung her pants in the closet. Tomorrow I'll have to tell Ginny. Tomorrow she'll be surprised to hear about Sandy and me.

Beth yawned. She took her pink pajamas from the drawer and slipped them on. After washing up, she took her diary from its secret place.

Dear Diary,

Tonight. . .

CHAPTER SEVEN

The Magic Formula

Beth wore her blue denim skirt and a blue-checked cotton blouse with rolled-up sleeves which were held up by tiny button tabs. It was one of her favorite blouses. She wondered if Sandy would notice she was wearing it.

The air was warm and the wind soft. She sang to herself as she walked down the hill toward school.

She was early that morning. Ginny had been away on Sunday, and Beth hadn't told her about the show and Sandy. She was going to wait for her friend, but for some reason she found herself walking. I hope she comes early today too, thought Beth as she turned in to the school-yard walk.

At the locker she gathered her morning-class books into a neat pile, then combed her hair.

"You should have waited. I stopped by your house so we could walk together." Ginny arrived out of breath. She tossed her windblown hair back and hung her red sweater in the locker, then she began to sort her books. When she stood up and turned toward

Beth, her mouth opened and her eyes widened. "You look terrific today," she said. "Is that new lipgloss?"

"No." Beth smiled and peered at herself in the mirror. Her cheeks were tinged pink, and her eyes looked deeper blue than usual. "I guess it's a combination," she said.

"A combination of what?" asked Ginny. "What's the magic formula?"

"Spring," said Beth, "and. . ."

"And? Tell me. You have a secret."

"And, I went to the show Saturday night with—"

"Beth, I can't stand this. Stop teasing." Ginny pretended to tear her hair.

"Guess."

"With Matt Morrow?"

"Wrong! With Sandy Grange."

Ginny stopped smiling. Her hands dropped down to her sides. "Sandy! Are you serious?"

"I went out with him only once. After we go skating next weekend, I'll let you know." Never before had Beth been so quick with words. She hoped she could be the same way when she talked with Sandy that day.

"Beth. . ."

Beth didn't answer. Sandy and his group were coming down the hall. He was wearing blue that day too. He threw his head back and laughed, then leaned down and whispered to Elsa. She punched him on the arm. He pretended to be hurt.

Beth smiled as she watched and waited for him to see her. But Pam called to him from farther down the hall, and he hurried by.

"You always did have a vivid imagination, Beth," said Ginny. "You almost had me believing you. Who really took you out Saturday night?"

"I didn't make it up," said Beth. "Sandy and I did go to the show. Ask Matt. He was there. He saw me with Sandy."

"Maybe I will," said Ginny. "But even if it is true, Sandy isn't interested in you as a girlfriend, Beth. I don't know why he asked you out, but you'd better wonder—if he really did."

"Thanks a lot for the insult." Beth slammed the locker door without asking Ginny if she had everything. "You know what I think? I think you're jealous, Ginny."

"Jealous! Me? Beth, you're kidding. I'm your friend."

"You were my friend. And I'm not kidding. From the first time I mentioned Sandy you've put him down. Well, I got another note at the library, and we're going skating Sunday. So keep your opinions to yourself."

Ginny's face flushed. She stared at Beth, then turned and spun the locker combination. "If that's what you think, Beth," she said in a tight, quiet voice, "I won't say another word to you about Sandy or about anything else." She yanked open the locker door, took out two books, slammed the door, and hurried away down the hall. She didn't look back once.

"With all the boys she knows, I don't know why she should care about the one that I go out with," said Beth softly. She felt very alone, though, as she started down the hall to her class.

"Beth, Beth, wait."

Beth stopped and looked back.

Sandy dodged through the hall crowd. When he reached her, he rested one shoulder against the lockers. He smiled as he looked down at her. The sight of him made Beth forget about Ginny and the words between them. "Have lunch with me today?" he asked. "I'll meet you outside drama class."

"Sure, Sandy."

"Good. See you at noon," he said. He was gone.

Beth reached up and touched the locker where his shoulder had rested. She expected it to be warm, but it wasn't. That'll show Ginny, she thought. I'll be sitting with Sandy's crowd at noon, and she'll be sorry she didn't believe me.

As Beth started to class, she hummed *Oklahoma!* songs under her breath.

Until she reached drama class, the morning dragged. Beth kept thinking about lunch. She couldn't remember what she'd packed that morning. If it's anything noisy like carrots or smelly like hard-boiled eggs, I'll say I'm not hungry, she thought. She looked over at Sandy.

"Mid-semester tests aren't that far off now, class. The week after grades are sent, we'll audition. Next week sign-up sheets will be posted for all roles and crews. Auditions will be scheduled for noon recesses. If your grades are too low, change your selection before I set up the schedule." Mr. Jordan took off his glasses and sat on the edge of his desk. "Joan Kaminski and Matt Morrow, come up and read Curly and Laurey, please.'' He called several others to read supporting parts.

''Now sing 'People Will Say We're In Love.' ''

Beth wondered what Sandy was thinking as she listened to the words of the song.

Joan's voice was soft and true. She had a little bit of trouble with the higher register though.

Everyone was amazed at Matt's voice. Not even a whisper could be heard in the class as he sang. He was so good, Beth saw Curly up there instead of Matt. She was surprised.

But Sandy looks more the part, she thought, feeling guilty. She looked to see if she could see his reaction.

He was resting his chin on one hand and looked bored.

The bell rang. Immediately Matt was surrounded by a crowd. ''You were good,'' said Beth as she squeezed past him. There was no harm in complimenting him, even if Sandy would probably get the role, she thought.

''Thanks, Beth,'' said Matt.

After this, thought Beth, I bet a lot of girls will notice Matt. She looked back at him for a minute before hurrying out of the classroom.

In the hall Sandy lounged against the lockers. No one else waited with him. Beth guessed they'd meet the others in the lunchroom.

''Let's get out of here. We'll eat in my car,'' said Sandy. ''It's warm outside.''

''Oh. All right.'' Beth felt disappointed and wondered if he noticed. She could hear it in her voice.

Now Ginny wouldn't see them together. She'd been one of the first to rush out of drama class, so there wasn't even the chance she'd seen them in the hall.

They stopped by Beth's locker so she could get her lunch. When she peeked inside, she saw a ham sandwich, a hard-boiled egg, an orange, and an apple muffin. She decided to eat the sandwich and the muffin.

Outside the sun was bright and warm. Spring was in the air. Other couples were leaving school to eat outdoors too. Some of them held hands.

I wish I had the nerve to take Sandy's hand, thought Beth. Her fingers tingled, but she didn't reach out to him.

"It's a beautiful day," she said.

"Yeah." Sandy opened the car door. Beth got in. "I want to ask you something. Don't answer, Beth, until I finish," he said.

The sun warmed the dark leather car seats. Sandy took her hand and squeezed it before he let go.

We're like the other couples, thought Beth happily. She turned toward Sandy ready to tell him how much his library notes meant to her; how she'd treasure them forever.

He took a white slip of paper from his pocket and handed it to her.

She opened it, expecting to see the familiar printing and the special signature, S. W. A. K. (Sealed With A Kiss). Instead, black printing from a school form spread its message across the paper. It was a Notice to Parents.

This is to inform you that your son, Alexander Grange, is presently maintaining a D average in advanced algebra. Please call my office for a consultation on this matter.

William Birch

"Mr. Birch gave me that today," said Sandy angrily. "Just what I needed, a D notice in math." He hit the steering wheel with his fist. "Now you have to help me, Beth. You can find the time for a couple of weeks. I need a crash course now."

Maybe it's too soon for him to talk to me about the notes, thought Beth, unable to let go of her earlier hope.

"Beth, say you'll help me."

"But when?" she asked, tucking the remembrance of the notes into the back of her mind and giving Sandy her full attention. "The library—"

"I know about the library." He sighed. "How about during lunch hour? Like you said, when I asked you before. We could work in the car. The weather is nice. Say you will, Beth."

His dark eyes pleaded, and he took her hand again. His skin was warm like the sun. His fingers were long and tan.

"All right," said Beth. "I'll try." She was aware of her own beating heart.

"Great!" A smile lit his face. "We'll start tomorrow." He pulled the note from between her fingers, crumpled it and tossed it over his shoulder. "No sense getting the old man's blood pressure up. I have confidence in you, Beth. We'll make beautiful music together in *Oklahoma!*"

They ate lunch. Beth's ham sandwich was dry and tasteless. She was worried that she wouldn't be very much help to him.

Sandy tuned the radio to the local rock station. He beat time to the music on the steering wheel, sometimes singing along with the record.

I'll be spending every afternoon with him, thought Beth. I shouldn't worry. I should be happy.

If only she and Ginny hadn't argued. She should have kept her opinions to herself. If it hadn't been for her, Beth's day would be perfect.

CHAPTER EIGHT

The New Igloo

Dear Diary,

I'm waiting for Sandy to pick me up. We're going skating at The New Igloo Ice Skating Rink. In case I don't have time to write later, I'm

Someone knocked on the bedroom door. Quickly Beth dropped her diary into the secret place, slid the drawer in, then called, "Come in."

"Beth, please come down to the study for a minute. Your father and I want to talk with you," said her mother. Frown lines creased her usually smooth forehead.

Beth wondered if something had happened to their book contract. It was the only thing that ever made her mother look that worried.

"Sandy will be here soon," she said.

"This won't take long." Her mother waited for her by the door.

Beth picked up her purse and sweater. Her feet

were warm from the double socks she wore. She didn't want to get blisters from skating. The last time she'd gone, when her family had visited their cousins in Minnesota, she'd gotten terrible sores on her ankles. She still remembered how they hurt.

The study was quiet as Beth and her mother entered. The lamps cast soft shadows in the room. Her father pushed his chair away from the desk.

"Sit down, Beth," he said. His voice was stern. So was his face.

Beth dropped down onto the edge of the couch. Part of her listened for Sandy's car, the other part listened to her father.

He removed his glasses, then turned his chair to face her. Her mother sat on the couch beside her. Beth sensed her tension.

"This boy you're waiting for, is he the same one who took you to the show, Beth?" her father asked.

"Yes. Sandy."

"Why didn't he come inside to meet us? Doesn't he have proper manners?" He came right to the point.

They've waited a whole week to ask me about Sandy's manners? Why does my father suddenly care now? wondered Beth. "It's not that," she said quickly. "We were late for the show, and he drives in all the way from the beach."

"That isn't an excuse, Beth. We expect to meet him tonight, or you won't be going anywhere."

She opened her mouth to reply, but her father continued.

"Also, he seems to have a very noisy car. Either that or he drives too fast." He stared at Beth until she looked down at her hands.

"Sandy knows what he's doing. He's been driving since—since last year," she finished softly. "He has his own car."

"Then, I repeat, you aren't to leave this house tonight until we meet him. A nice, polite boy doesn't honk the horn in front. He comes to the door. That's the proper way, Beth."

She felt reduced to a two-year-old state. Something exploded inside of her. "You're living in the Middle Ages. Things are different now. No one bows or curtsies. Sometimes the girls even pick up the boys." Her voice sounded loud in the study. When she stopped talking, the tick-tock of the grandfather clock seemed to scold.

Her father's face tightened. His usually soft mouth was a hard, straight line. "But the girls don't sit out front and honk their horns."

Beth couldn't argue, because she'd never met any girls who drove their boyfriends.

"You see, Beth, manners aren't different," said her father. "Good ones never go out of style."

Beth looked at her mother hoping for help. All this time she'd been sure her father didn't notice or care what she did. She was wrong. Now that Sandy was taking her out, he seemed to care too much. Beth squirmed on the couch and strained her ears for the sound of the red car. They're going to spoil everything for me, she thought. I bet Elsa's parents don't lecture her.

She jumped as the quick beep-beep of a horn sounded out in front.

"Don't leave," said her father, standing also.

"Dad, you live in this old-fashioned house and have old-fashioned ideas. I'm old enough to decide where I'll go, when I'll go, how I'll go, and with whom."

"Beth," said her mother. Shock and warning sounded in her voice.

Beth's father stared at her.

I've challenged him a second time, she thought nervously. Her stomach knotted. What would he do?

The silence was broken by the ringing of the doorbell. Tears pressed behind Beth's eyes. Why did he have to pick that night to discuss it? It wasn't fair. The bell rang again.

Her father strode out of the study. His movement sent Beth hurrying behind him. In the hall she rushed around him and reached the front door first. Quickly she opened it.

"Beth, didn't you hear—?" began Sandy. His smile faded as he seemed to understand the situation inside the house.

"Invite the young man in," said Beth's father from behind her. Neither his words nor his tone of voice were welcoming. He'd given an order, not an invitation.

Beth swallowed what she thought an appropriate comment about manners and looked pleadingly at Sandy.

He shrugged and stepped into the entry hall. He was wearing designer blue jeans and a burgundy velour shirt.

My parents can't complain about his appearance, thought Beth proudly.

Her mother had come from the study also. She

stood next to Beth's father. Unity in action.

"Mom, Dad, this is Sandy Grange. Sandy, these are my parents, Mr. and Mrs. Winston." Now I hope we can leave, she thought.

"Hi," said Sandy. He shook hands with Beth's father and nodded quickly to her mother. Then he turned to Beth. "Are you ready?" he asked.

"Yes," she said and started out the door, anxious to leave.

"Remember, you have school tomorrow," called her mother.

"Yes, and drive carefully, young man. Keep your mind on your driving and your hands on the wheel."

Beth wanted to die right there. Why did her father have to say *that?* "Let's go, Sandy," she said, hurrying down the porch steps and onto the walk as fast as possible. She didn't look back.

When they were in the car, she glanced at Sandy. "I'm sorry. My dad is kind of old-fashioned."

"No big deal," said Sandy.

I hope he means it, thought Beth.

He started the motor. The tires screeched as the car pulled away from the front of the house. Beth could imagine what her father was saying. Her face must have reflected her thoughts.

"Hey, don't worry," said Sandy. "See? My hands are on the wheel." He laughed.

Beth forced a half smile. "It's because I'm the only one," she said. "My parents don't see me as grown up. They're overprotective."

"Grown up," said Sandy. "My parents don't care if I'm ten or two hundred. They only want me to get into a good college and learn to make a lot of money so they can brag and look good."

Beth thought that his parents sounded uncaring. "Do you know where you want to go or what you want to study?" she asked.

"I don't care where I go, and I want to study girls." Sandy turned the car into the skating rink parking lot.

Brightly colored streamers stretched across the front of the white stucco building. A Kleig searchlight tilted its high-power beam back and forth across the sky, advertising the presence of The New Igloo Ice Skating Rink.

Beth and Sandy pushed open the heavy glass doors. The rink was crowded. The organ music made Beth feel as if she could glide like a skating star. She was anxious to get on the ice. It would be wonderful to skate with Sandy's arm around her waist.

While Sandy paid the admission, Beth admired the skating outfits on display in the shop window. One leotard was royal blue. The skirt had alternating light and royal blue panels. Beth wondered how it would look on her.

"Come on," said Sandy.

They got skates from the counter inside, then sat on a long wooden bench. Beth slipped off her shoes. Sandy, next to her, quickly donned his own skates. It seemed to take Beth forever to crisscross the ties and catch all the white hooks. Sandy was ready before she was.

"Hurry up," he said standing and pacing on thin, silver blades.

A short girl with long, red hair skated up to the wooden half wall that separated the ice from the sitting area. She wore a green skating outfit with matching tights.

I wish I had a short skirt to wear instead of jeans, thought Beth, admiring the girl's outfit.

"Hi, Sandy," she said. "Want to skate?"

He turned to Beth. "I'll try the ice with Kathy," he said. "Be back in a second."

Beth was almost ready, but he was gone before she could stand up. Her feet felt stiff. She could barely move her toes. She wobbled a bit as she started toward the wall.

Sandy and Kathy glided by. He held her tightly around the waist. Their feet moved in smooth, rhythmic strides.

Other skaters stroked by at varying speeds around the edge of the ice. Parents with small children between them looked as if they were having fun. In the center of the rink, two girls held hands and tried to spin in a circle. Another skated on one foot, while a boy practiced jumps. They all made skating look easy.

Sandy and Kathy passed a second time. Beth raised her hand and waved, but Sandy didn't seem to notice.

"Beth, I didn't know you liked to skate." Matt glided to a stop on the ice and leaned on the wall opposite her. He wore a red and blue ski sweater and old blue jeans.

"I'm not very good," she said.

"Neither am I, but I work at it. Sometimes tall people have to make an effort to look coordinated. When the rink opened, I decided this was a good place for my effort." He smiled.

"You never look uncoordinated to me," she blurted out, then felt her face burn. It seemed like a dumb thing to say.

"Thanks. Shows my efforts are paying off," said Matt. "Would you like to skate with me?"

Beth hesitated. Part of her wanted to say yes, but what would Sandy say?

She didn't have time to worry about that. Sandy skidded to a stop next to Matt. Kathy wasn't with him anymore. A spray of ice spattered through the break in the wall and onto the floor. "Are your skates adjusted, Beth?" he asked, ignoring Matt.

"Yes, I'm ready." She smiled at Matt, then stepped out on the ice.

Matt skated off across the rink. Beth stood still and watched him for a minute.

"Let's go," said Sandy impatiently. He took her hand.

After the first couple of strides, her ankles bent like wet spaghetti. "This isn't as easy as it looks," she said. She grabbed for the wall and missed. She tried to keep her balance and held on to Sandy's arm, but suddenly she was on the ice and had pulled Sandy down with her.

"Way to go," called someone skating by.

Beth couldn't look at Sandy. She was too embarrassed.

"Need some lessons, Sandy?" someone else called.

"Never saw you fall like that for any girl before," said another voice.

Beth crawled to the wall and pulled herself up. She wished Sandy's friends would stop teasing. She hadn't meant to pull him down with her.

Sandy was already on his feet, brushing ice powder and slush from his jeans. He didn't say anything, but he wasn't smiling either.

Beth wished she could think of a joking remark, anything to lighten the moment; but her mind was blank.

"Maybe if I go along the wall for a little way, my feet will remember." She tried to make light of her awkwardness.

"I don't care," said Sandy. "Go ahead." He skated backward while she half walked, half staggered, half fell around the rink. Why did I ever think I could skate? she wondered, feeling miserable and conspicuous. And why didn't Sandy help?

"Come on," said Sandy as they came around to the break in the wall. "Let's sit down for a few minutes. You look like you need a rest."

"I'm not a very good skater," said Beth. "I guess it's been too long. I've forgotten how."

"Yeah," said Sandy. "You should have mentioned that when I asked you."

"I didn't know it would matter," said Beth, feeling angry and hurt. Sandy helped her off the ice. They sat in the first two spectator seats behind the wall.

"Hey, Beth, Sandy, are you two getting too old to skate?" Two girls from school, Beth didn't know either of them very well, stopped by the wall. "Poor Sandy, can't keep up," they teased.

"Go on and skate," said Beth. "I'll try again in a few minutes."

Across the rink she saw Matt skating slowly alone.

He didn't do anything fancy, but had a steady, confident stride. She'd try to imitate him.

"Maybe I should take you home," said Sandy. "Your old man will probably have a rut worn in the floor worrying about you."

"He's not as strict as he seems." Beth didn't want to leave yet. She wanted to master the art of ice skating.

"You could have fooled me. He looked like he wanted to roast me alive when I picked you up tonight. Let's go. There's no one here tonight anyway." Sandy pulled the laces on his skates.

Beth sighed, but she didn't argue. The whole evening had been totally awful.

Sandy drove slowly as they headed back to central Fern Grove. Beth wished he would say something; tell her that he didn't mind that she didn't skate well; say that her father wouldn't scare him off.

Ginny's voice echoed in her head. *You're not his type*. She reached over and turned up the radio to block out these thoughts. Sandy was fun. He was exciting. He was taking her home early because he knew she wasn't having fun, because he didn't want her to get in trouble with her parents. Beth tried to convince herself, but suddenly she wished she hadn't argued with Ginny.

Sandy stopped the car in front of the house. "I'll see you at lunch tomorrow," he said. "I guess I'd better not walk you to the door. Your old man might be waiting."

"My father," said Beth. She got out of the car and started up the walk. Was Sandy really afraid of her father? Was that the reason he didn't walk her to the door? She wanted to think it was, but tiny doubts flickered inside her. No matter how she tried to allay them, they refused to go. He'll never ask me out again, she thought, I just know it. She didn't know why it mattered so much, but it did. She felt awful.

CHAPTER NINE

Doing Battle

Beth didn't want to see her parents when she went inside. She opened the front door as quietly as possible. The television was on. Her father laughed at whatever program he and her mother were watching.

In imitation of Zorro when he stalked a mouse, Beth carefully snuck up to her room, taking care to avoid any steps that might creak and give notice that she was there.

At the top of the stairs, she moved a little faster, turned right, stepped into her bedroom, closed the door quietly, then exhaled. All that time she'd been holding her breath.

I would never make a good burglar, she thought. Surely I'd pass out from lack of oxygen before I could manage to burgle anything.

In her room she felt safe from questions. She could imagine the kind her father would ask. *Didn't your friend like coming to the house for you? Did he keep his hands on the wheel? Why did he bring you home so early?*

If Beth was lucky, her parents wouldn't check her room until they came up to bed. They wouldn't know how long she'd been home.

For once she wished their house were even more old-fashioned, old enough to have bedroom washstands. But it had modern plumbing despite the old pipes. She decided to wait awhile before venturing to the bathroom to wash up. That would be a sure signal to her parents that she was home.

She slipped out of her jeans and sweater and into her green granny nightgown. Turning back the multi-colored patchwork quilt, Beth crawled into the middle of her bed.

If she looked sideways, she could see herself in the cheval glass that stood near the closet. That night it reflected a puzzled Beth. She went over and over the evening at the skating rink, trying to decide what had gone wrong. Was it her fault? Her parents' fault? Sandy's fault? She felt mixed-up and confused.

Giving up, she crawled off her bed and took her diary from its place in the desk. Then she stretched out on the bed once more to complete the entry she'd started earlier. When Beth had begun, she thought she wouldn't have time to complete it. Now she had the time but couldn't think of the right words to record her evening. She rested her head on her arm to think.

Beth started and woke up. Wind, blowing from the ocean, shook the trees growing at the side of the house. One long branch scratched its needles at the bedroom window as if it wanted to come inside.

Her diary was on the cover next to her. She'd

fallen asleep and never completed her entry.

Her room felt damp and cool. She closed the diary, slipped it under her pillow, then pulled the blankets around herself.

Minutes later there was a light knock on her bedroom door. She closed her eyes and pretended to be asleep. Beth heard the door open.

"She's home and in bed," said her mother. Surprise and relief sounded in her voice.

"But when did she come in?" asked her father. "It's midnight now. Why didn't she tell us?"

"In the morning we'll ask her."

Beth could imagine her mother's hand on her father's arm as he stepped toward the bed to waken her. He probably thought she'd been very late.

The door clicked shut. Beth half opened her eyes to be sure they'd gone. Now she'd have to wait until the morning to wash. And in the morning she'd have to explain that she wasn't late and why she didn't tell them she was home. Would they possibly understand? She wasn't sure she did.

Beth closed her eyes again but couldn't sleep. The wind blew harder, whistling around the edges of the house. Her eyelids lifted, and she stared into the darkness while she waited for morning to come.

"What time did you come in last night?" Her father thumped his coffee cup down and asked the question before Beth was seated at the breakfast table.

She sat down, reached for the box of Raisin Bran, and poured some into the bowl before she answered. "I wasn't late," she said.

"That wasn't the question."

She could feel him staring at her. She tried to count the raisins.

"Beth!"

"I'm not sure what time. I didn't look at the clock. You weren't in bed," she said hurriedly.

As soon as she said the last, she knew there would be more questions. It might have been better if I had stayed outside until it was late and come in then, she thought, taking a spoonful of cereal.

"Then why didn't you tell us you were home? We didn't hear you come in, and your mother and I were worried. If she hadn't thought to look in your room, we might still be waiting for you—or called the sheriff."

"The sheriff! Why would you do that?" Beth put her spoon down.

"Something could have happened to you. That boy isn't the safest driver in Fern Grove, that's obvious." Her father's voice was sarcastic.

"Nothing happened," she said, hearing the defensiveness in her words. "I can take care of myself. I always have."

"But, Beth," said her mother, "why didn't you tell us you were home?" She'd been listening and observing from beside the sink where she peeled potatoes for a stew.

"You were busy. I was tired. I just didn't," said Beth.

"We weren't busy. If you came in early, you must have heard the television," said her mother.

"And were you so tired you couldn't have said good night to us before going to bed?" Her father glared at her over his coffee cup.

Beth felt alone in her own house. Suddenly there was a wall between her parents and herself—a wall that had never been there before. A line had been drawn. They had their side and she had hers.

She poured milk into a glass and took a sip. It had no taste. There seemed to be a lump in her throat when she tried to swallow.

"We do not approve of this boy, Sandy, who has been taking you out, Beth," said her father.

"Why?"

"He isn't your kind."

This was Ginny all over again. "What is my kind? You don't like him because he's rich."

"Is he rich?" asked her father.

"I told you that he lives at the beach."

"Not everyone who lives at the beach is rich," said her mother. "Some of the families who live there were in their homes before it became a fashionable place to build."

Beth didn't know that, but she didn't admit it.

"We'd prefer that you don't go out with Sandy again," said her father.

"That should be my decision," said Beth. "Not yours."

"We only care about you." Her mother came and put a hand on Beth's shoulder.

Beth shook her off.

"We wouldn't say this if we didn't think—" began her mother again.

"You don't even know Sandy." Beth stood up. "One meeting and you've made up your mind. Well, I'm sorry. If I want to go out with him, I will, whether you like him or not."

Her father jumped up, sending his chair scraping across the floor. His eyes were bright and his face flushed. Beth had never seen him look as angry as he did at that moment.

Her mother moved to his side. She placed a hand on his arm. "Perhaps Beth is right. She must make the decisions about her friends," she said. "We have no reason to mistrust her. She's always done well on her own."

"Thanks," said Beth. Her appetite had gone. "I'd better get to school." She ran to her room and gathered her books. She grabbed her jacket from the closet.

"Have a good day at school," called her mother as Beth came back downstairs. She spoke as if it were a normal day.

"Yeah." I sound like Sandy, thought Beth. He says yeah. It isn't my word.

Outside the wind was still gusting. Spring had been temporarily blown away. As she walked down the hill to school, Beth thought about her morning. She felt she'd won the battle with her parents. Her mother had conceded her right to choose friends. Beth should have felt victorious. Instead, she had a dull, empty feeling inside. I'll feel better at noon when I see Sandy, she thought.

The library was closed because of a budget meeting. Mrs. Forest was hoping to get more money for books. She had gone to plead her case in person.

Beth had offered to work alone, but Mrs. Forest had said no. "Take the day off too," she'd said.

"You work every day after school, Beth. You deserve some time."

Now Beth had her day off but didn't want to go home. She couldn't decide where else to go either.

To kill time she walked down to the shops in Fern Grove. There weren't many, but the few that were there were interesting. Four were dress shops. There was a complete drugstore, The Play House, a live theatre, also a medical center, an auto repair shop, the cleaners, the grocery, and The General Store.

The General Store was an old-fashioned gift shop. It sold almost everything. Inside it smelled of cedar and spice. It had wooden floors, oak counters, and even a potbellied stove, which was never lit, however.

Beth went inside to browse. There were some antique dolls on display. She stopped to study them. They had porcelain faces and beautiful glass eyes. Their clothes were of silks, satins, and handmade lace.

In her closet at home, she had a French doll that had belonged to her great-grandmother. The doll had never been played with. Beth's mother would never let her dress or undress the doll, only look at her. Beth remembered feeling very sorry for the doll, because she thought the doll must have wanted to be cuddled and loved but never could be because she was too beautiful.

How ironic, she thought, looking at the dolls in the display case. A doll may be too beautiful to love, but often a person is too plain to love.

She turned away from the display to look at jewelry. Why should she be thinking such depressing thoughts? Surely she was loved. Sandy had said Beth was his girl. He'd said so the night at the show. At noon that day he'd held her hand. He hadn't mentioned the skating rink.

I would like to invite him over, but now I'm afraid to, thought Beth, wandering to a stationery rack. My father isn't good at hiding his feelings. He might spoil any chance I have of staying Sandy's girl. I'm having enough trouble by myself. Maybe when I've been going out with him for a while, my father will change his mind.

"Let's go in The General Store for a minute. I want to buy some of those cute printed shoelaces for my tennis shoes. They have the purple ones with unicorns on them."

Beth recognized Ginny's voice. She came through the entrance with Joan.

"Hi, Beth," called Joan as Beth hurried past them toward the door.

"Hi," she mumbled as she hurried out and kept on going. She hadn't known that Ginny and Joan were friends. She felt very alone. Ginny, her father—they would all see. Sandy wasn't the way they thought he was. Why would he have asked her out if he didn't care about her? Why would he have sent the notes? He wanted to know her better. He must think I'm his type, no matter what Ginny or anyone else thinks, decided Beth.

With her head high, she started toward home.

CHAPTER TEN

Down to the Wire

Mid-semester tests started the next day. On the following Monday auditions would begin. Beth sighed out loud as she thought of how quickly the time had passed.

"Quadratics, variables, logs, *x*, *y*, *z*! I hate this garbage!" Sandy shut the book and turned on the radio.

"We aren't finished," said Beth. She took the book from him and opened it to the page where they'd been working.

"You aren't. I am." He flipped the radio knob to off and climbed out of the car. "See you later, Beth."

She wished he'd try harder, but that day she didn't call him back. There wasn't much more she could help him with anyway. Instead she settled back in the car seat and took the time to study for herself. Explaining math to Sandy should have made the subject clearer to her, but working with Sandy had been distracting and sometimes frustrating. Frustration seemed to be all she retained from their study sessions.

Sandy had never mentioned the rink, and neither had he asked Beth out again. They spent each lunch hour together, however. He wasn't easy to get to know. When Beth had tried to speak of anything serious besides math, he changed the subject or decided he'd had enough studying. She wished he would talk to her. She couldn't even tell him about her parents. He wouldn't take the time to listen.

But she couldn't stay angry with him for very long. When she was angry, he would charm her out of it and promise to behave. He'd beg her not to give up their lunches together. He was like a little boy, charming but impossible.

He didn't know that Beth worried about her own grades. English, where she'd always pulled an A, had dropped to a B.

She felt this was partly her parents' fault. The tension at home was bad. Her father hadn't forgiven her for calling him old-fashioned. But she still thought he was and wouldn't apologize for speaking the truth. They had a cold truce.

Beth's mother tried to play intermediary between them, but nothing changed. They spoke of neutral subjects.

Beth's dream of playing Laurey in *Oklahoma!* seemed to be fading. She'd read the drama class lists that day. There were ten girls signed up for the part of Laurey. Only six boys were trying out for Curly. Two of them were Matt and Sandy.

"Where's your star pupil?"

Beth turned to see Ginny standing next to the car.

She wondered how long she'd been there. They saw each other at their locker but rarely spoke.

"We're finished," said Beth. "I was just doing a little studying of my own."

"Mind if I sit in the car with you?"

"No." Beth was surprised at her request. Was it lecture time again? she wondered.

But for a while Ginny sat quietly. "Beth. . ."

"Ginny. . ."

They both spoke at the same time.

"I'm sorry." Echoes again.

"I should have kept my opinions to myself. It isn't my business who takes you out," said Ginny.

"I shouldn't be so touchy. We've been best friends too long to stay angry. Friends again?" asked Beth.

"Friends forever," said Ginny. "Are you nervous about next week?"

"I'm more nervous about this week. There's so much to study. What if I don't get C's? Then I won't have to worry about next week." Beth felt relieved telling someone about her fear.

"You'll do fine," said Ginny.

"I'm not so sure about algebra."

"We could study together tonight."

"You wouldn't mind? That's always helped before. I'll come down to your house. My parents are busy with their book, and the typewriters are going constantly." She didn't tell Ginny the real reason she preferred to get out of the house.

"Sure. Come after dinner," said Ginny.

"All right. Thanks."

The bell sounded for the end of lunch period. The

two friends left the car and walked together to their locker.

"I'm glad we aren't fighting any more," said Beth, as they went into school. "I've missed our friendship."

"Me too," said Ginny.

Beth felt better at that moment than she had in a long while. She really hadn't realized how important Ginny's friendship was to her.

Ginny's house was a modern tri-level of redwood and glass. It was tall and narrow with second-story decks all around. In the summer Beth and Ginny sometimes sunbathed on the deck. They lay on towels and listened to the radio. From up there, they could watch the beach traffic go by on the street below.

The last summer Ginny had called and waved to boys in cars as they drove past. Beth had waved sometimes too, but she never said anything. Ginny had said she wished her mother grew roses. "With a name like ours, we should have a whole garden," she'd say jokingly. "If we had roses, Ginny Rose could throw flowers down to the cutest boys."

Beth rang the doorbell.

Mrs. Rose answered the door. She had silvery hair, styled very neatly. She always wore skirts and round-collared blouses. Beth had never seen her wear jeans. "Hello, Beth," she said. "Come in." She stepped back. "Ginny is in her room. Just head for the noise."

The radio was blasting the Go-Go's latest hit. Climbing the carpeted stairs always seemed strange to Beth. She was used to hearing her feet tap on wood.

Ginny's room was to the left. Since the last time Beth had visited, the room had been redecorated. Now it was violet, Ginny's current favorite color. The rug was still off-white, but the walls were violet, the spreads on the twin brass beds were violet flowered, and the trim on the white curtains was violet. It was a good color on Ginny, but Beth thought she'd get tired of so much of it. She kept her opinion to herself, however—one lesson she'd learned.

"Come in," called Ginny over the stream of words from the radio disc jockey. "I've redecorated. Isn't this neat? The only thing missing is that unicorn poster down at The General Store. As soon as I have enough saved, I'm going to buy it and have it framed and hang it on the wall right between the beds." She was stretched out on the floor with books all around her.

"Looks fine," said Beth. She dropped her books onto the twin bed that she and Ginny had always called hers.

"I'd love a violet telephone, too, but they don't make one. Mom says I can trade my blue one for a white one, though. That will look better." Ginny rolled over on her back and put both hands behind her head. "Did you see the spring dance posters at school?"

"No." Beth dropped down on the floor too.

"The dance is next weekend. Guess who asked me to go?"

"Bob Roserman."

"I should be so lucky. He'll probably ask Joan."

"Did Kevin ask you?"

"Don't I wish."

"Then who?"

"Eddie MacIntyre."

"Really? Eddie is one of Sandy's friends. Are you going?"

"I can't." Ginny wrinkled her nose and twisted her mouth into a crooked line.

"Why?"

"My parents won't let me. And I guess I really don't mind so much. My dad hears which kids the sheriff has trouble with. I don't dare mention any of them around here."

"You mean you have to ask if you can go out? I always thought your parents let you decide."

"They do. But they've made it known which boys better not show up here. They always meet whoever takes me out." She raised her head and looked at Beth for a minute. "Eddie, Sandy, and most the kids in that crowd are on the 'bad guys' list."

"When did all this happen? You never mentioned it before."

"It's always been. None of those guys ever asked me out until Eddie."

"That doesn't seem fair," said Beth. "You should be able to choose whomever you want to date."

"Maybe. But I listened to Gail on this one. Having an older sister is a big plus, Beth. When Gail was home last time, she told me, 'Don't give Mom and Dad a hard time about the few restrictions they give you, and you'll get away with almost everything else.' And it's true; I do."

"Yeah," said Beth. She pulled her books from the bed and spread them on the floor.

"Anyway I don't care if I go to this dance or if I go out with Eddie. I'm still working on Kevin." She rolled back onto her stomach and shuffled the pages in her algebra book.

"We'd better get our studying done," said Beth. Their discussion was making her uncomfortable. She thought it was unfair for parents to judge boys on hearsay. But she didn't want to fight with Ginny again. Besides, Ginny had lots of boys calling her. Beth didn't. Her one boyfriend was Sandy. Would Ginny listen to Gail if that was her situation? Beth didn't ask.

Monday had come and the grades were handed out. Beth got all B's except for a C in math. What a relief!

The sign-up sheet in drama class had several black lines drawn on it. The ten girls were down to seven for Laurey. Only two boys were left under Curly—Matt and Sandy.

"You must have done all right in math," said Beth as Sandy came to the board to read the list also. What would happen now that their lunch-hour studying was over? she wondered.

Sandy grinned. "No sweat. I pulled a C-minus. I think Mr. Birch knew how much I needed that grade." He looked at the list again. "Looks like I'll have the lead for sure. Morrow isn't real competition."

"He has a good voice," said Beth.

"Sure, teach," said Sandy, "but so do I." He

looked down at her through long, thick dark lashes. "And I've got the experience." He moved over to scan the girls' list, then turned back toward Beth. "Speaking of experience, there's a dance Friday night. Want to go?"

"The spring dance?" said Beth. "I'd love to." He still wanted to be with her. Some of the doubts she'd had melted away.

"Good. I'll take you." Sandy winked at her, then went back to his desk.

Beth walked slowly to hers as Mr. Jordan came into the room. My dream might come true, she thought. Sandy and I could be the leads in *Oklahoma!*

"Attention, class," said Mr. Jordan. "Girls, you will begin auditions this afternoon during lunch. I'll number the list and mark your day and time. Boys will follow when I've finished with the girls. I'll announce the roles a week from today; then, it's down to work. Rehearsals, at noon and after school and possibly some weekends. Crews meet here after school tomorrow."

Beth was worried about her library job. Maybe she should cross her name off the list now. But the songs and lines were a part of her. She was Laurey. She had to try out for the part.

Sandy waited for her after class. "We'll make a great team," he said. "Right?"

"And get better acquainted?" Beth hoped the phrase from the note would show him she knew he'd written them.

"If that's what you want, Beth," he said. "You can start calling me Curly right now."

"Ready for lunch, Beth?" asked Ginny.

Beth looked at Sandy, thinking maybe he'd ask her to eat with him.

"See you later." He winked and moved off down the hall. He was joined by Elsa and Pam along the way.

"You'll get the part," said Ginny. "You and Matt."

"Or Sandy and I." Beth watched him as long as possible.

Ginny sighed but didn't comment.

CHAPTER ELEVEN

Spring Dance

Beth was surprised when her parents didn't make a fuss about the dance. Since she'd told them, she'd been waiting for the blowup. Nothing happened.

On Friday night Sandy arrived at the front door. He did all the right things—held her sweater, spoke to her parents, even promised not to be out too late. Beth hoped her parents noticed. They would see they were wrong about Sandy.

She'd chosen her pale blue skirt and a white, silky blouse to wear. At her neck was an enamel locket painted with tiny blue and yellow flowers, a gift from her grandmother.

The night was clear. The stars made a dotted-swiss pattern on dark navy. The moon cut an almost full circle out of the sky.

"Ready for the dance, Laurey?" asked Sandy.

"Sure, Curly," said Beth.

It was fun pretending they had the roles. In a few days they'd know for sure.

The school parking lot was jammed with cars. The

gym doors were open. Beth could hear the band warming up. She was looking forward to the dance. She wasn't a super dancer, but she did know the steps and being with Sandy would give her confidence.

Groups of kids were gathered inside the door and along the walls, the guys checking out the girls and vice versa. Beth had always been one of the kids in the girls' group when she'd attended the dances. How she'd envied girls coming through the doors with a special boy. Now she was one of them. It felt wonderful, especially when that boy was so handsome, like Sandy.

The dance theme was "A Spring Garden." Pastel streamers crisscrossed the gym ceiling. Paper lattices climbed the walls with tissue paper flowers and crepe paper vines attached.

As Beth looked toward the temporary stage set up beside the basketball net, she was surprised. The band was a radical rock group. THE CHAINS said the gold chain lettering on the huge black-and-gold drum set. The band members were all girls. Their costumes were half-black, half-gold leotards. Even their irregularly chopped heads of hair and faces were done in half-black, half-gold. Around their waists they wore gold chains. The girl Beth guessed to be the lead player wore a huge gold padlock around her neck. Beth wondered how she kept her neck from aching.

"All right!" shouted Sandy, making a thumbs-up sign. "For once we have a good band."

One of the girls smiled at him and kissed the air.

"See you later, babe," he called and laughed.

Beth didn't know what to say.

"Let's get a drink," he said, dragging Beth toward the table where the punch and soft drinks were for sale. He dropped two quarters on the table and handed her a glass of punch.

The band started its first song. Beth could feel the vibration of the music in the floor. Her feet itched to dance.

Sandy leaned close and shouted in her ear, "I have to talk to someone. Be back in a few minutes, Beth."

"Wait!" she said. The word was drowned out by the throb of the music. He was gone, and she'd feel silly chasing him across the gym.

Beth sipped her punch and tried to see where Sandy was going. He weaved in and out among the dancers. Beth tried to look as if she was having a good time by smiling at anyone she knew. All the while she watched Sandy.

Minutes later she saw him with Elsa in a darker part of the gym. Elsa was easy to spot with her distinctive hair and clothes. That night she wore a silky, hot pink jumpsuit with thin ties on each shoulder. She and Sandy talked at the edge of the dance floor, then he put his arm around her waist and led her into the middle of all the dancing couples. They twisted and rocked opposite each other, keeping perfect time to the beat of the music.

Beth tried to pretend she didn't care, but it was the skating rink all over—even worse. She hadn't even had a chance to dance with Sandy.

Looking up as the music ended, Beth hoped to see Sandy coming back toward her. Instead, he and Elsa were back in the same corner with Jill and Pam. Both girls wore jumpsuits similar to Elsa's. Jill's was white. Pam's was pale blue. Beth wished she'd worn something different.

Her punch was gone. She set the empty cup on the edge of the table and moved toward the row of chairs along the gym wall. She'd wait a little while. If Sandy didn't come back, she'd . . . She'd what? Beth was trying to decide what she'd do as she headed for an empty folding chair. Nothing made sense. If Sandy didn't want to be with her, why had he asked her to the dance?

Beth was thinking so hard, she bumped into someone. A firm hand grabbed her arm to keep her from falling. "Sorry," she muttered, too upset with Sandy to be embarrassed. Looking up she saw a familiar face.

Matt smiled at her. "We meet again," he said. "I hoped you'd be here."

Beth noticed he was wearing his "sandy" outfit. The colors were good on him.

"I'm not great at the fast dances," he said. "Want to sit and talk until something slower comes along?"

Beth let him lead her toward two vacant chairs.

"Have you had your audition yet?" he asked.

"Yesterday. I was scared to death. I think I mixed up a couple of lines, but the songs went perfectly."

"I had mine today. Don't know if I beat Grange out or not. Mr. Jordan doesn't give a hint."

"Oh. Sandy didn't even mention his audition," said Beth, wondering why.

For a minute Matt's smile faded. "Are you here with him tonight?"

"Sort of. He's talking to someone."

"Then you talk with me, and you'll be talking

with someone too," said Matt. "This is the first school dance I've ever attended. I decided I was getting too bookish and neglecting my social side. My kid sister, Lisa, told me I'd get old and crotchety if I didn't start having some fun." Matt smiled again. "The push for a college scholarship can do that to you. It's been pretty time consuming."

"You mean you've got one?"

"I think so, but it's not official yet. I can't do much more at this point except keep my grades up and participate. That was my weak spot. The schools look for well-rounded students. So now I'm rounding out my social side."

"Where do you think you'll be going to school?"

"The University of California, theatre major."

"You want to be in movies?" asked Beth.

"Behind the scenes. I want to learn it all—writing, directing, photography, makeup, et cetera. I figure I'll get some acting experience too, but that's not my ultimate goal. Eventually I want to produce and direct my own films."

"I envy you. I'm not sure what I want. Something to do with music. Maybe acting," said Beth, "possibly teaching or composing. It's so hard to know what you want to do with your whole life when you're only a junior in high school."

"Whatever you choose, you'll be successful. You're talented," said Matt. "I think you'll get the part of Laurey for sure."

"Oh, I hope so," said Beth, surprised by his compliments.

A slower song started. Sandy hadn't returned.

"Do you think Sandy would mind if you danced

with me?'' asked Matt.

''I don't mind,'' said Beth, smiling at him. Right then she didn't care what Sandy Grange minded.

After leading her onto the dance floor, Matt put his arm around her and pulled her close. Beth's head came up just under his chin, which was nice. With most boys she either looked them in the forehead or, if she was lucky, straight in the eye. Matt was a good dancer, smooth and steady like his skating; nothing too fancy. His sweater felt soft against her cheek. He smelled of lemon and spice.

He didn't talk while they danced and neither did Beth. It wasn't an uncomfortable silence though. For the first time since arriving at the dance, she felt relaxed.

As they moved on the edge of the crowded dance floor, Beth occasionally tried to spot Sandy; but he seemed to have disappeared into some other dark corner where he was invisible. She wondered if he'd left the dance without her. Beth was surprised that she didn't seem to care.

Another rock number started. ''I'm willing to try if you are,'' said Matt.

Beth admired Matt for attempting something he didn't feel comfortable with. She liked his honesty as well. He didn't try to be what he wasn't. That thought made her uncomfortable, but she wasn't sure why. Sandy was different from Matt, but she was sure he wasn't putting on an act.

''Why not!'' she said. ''Let's dance.''

They danced equally well, neither of them a prize winner in the rock category, but neither did so badly either.

Almost an hour passed before Sandy came looking for Beth. He brought her another glass of punch as the band took a break.

"Thank you for the dances, Beth," said Matt. He left her with Sandy.

"Got to talking and lost track of time," said Sandy.

"Yeah," she said imitating him. "I noticed."

"Hey, don't be mad." Sandy put his arm around her shoulders.

Beth pulled away. "I want to go home," she said.

"But the dance isn't over."

"It never started for me," said Beth. "I'll walk. You can stay and talk to your friends."

"No. Don't walk. I'll take you."

Beth could see him scanning the crowd over her shoulder.

"There's Eddie," he said. "I have to tell him one thing, then I'll be back." He was off again. "Wait for me," he called back over his shoulder.

The band climbed back on the stage, and the music began.

Beth didn't bother to look to see where Sandy was going this time. She looked for Matt. He was dancing with Joan. Beth finished her second glass of punch and headed for the girls' bathroom.

She read the graffiti in the middle stall, none of it very original. Some of it was crude, most of it dull. Combing her hair and putting on fresh lipgloss didn't take very long.

Sandy should be ready to leave, she thought, as she returned to the dance. As she came into the gym, there was a crowd standing around the edge of the floor. In the center were Sandy and Pam dancing to a wild rock number. Beth didn't want to watch. She went to the coat rack and found her sweater.

She pushed open one of the double doors just as the band announced that that number had been their closing one.

Immediately others began to leave. Beth was walking across the lot when Sandy caught up with her.

"A great dance," he said, offering her a mint candy.

Beth shook her head. "Was it?" She heard the icy tone in her voice but didn't care.

Sandy took her arm and guided her toward the car. Horns blared. There were shouts of laughter from various corners of the parking lot. Beth was quiet.

"Well, I had a great time," said Sandy. "If you didn't that's your fault, Beth. I did notice that Morrow danced with you." He opened the car door.

"I noticed that you didn't," said Beth. She was too angry for tears. She stared straight ahead.

Sandy laughed and messed her hair. "Cool off," he said. "The dance was over too soon. I would have danced with you if there was another set. I like you, Beth, but I'm a social guy. No one girl owns me. That's the way I am. I spread myself around—especially to those girls who keep me interested. I've got lots of girls. I take the special ones places, but that doesn't mean I'm tied to them."

Beth felt confused. He made it sound like she was making a big deal out of nothing. Had she expected too much? As they drove she tried to straighten out her thoughts.

Sandy whistled along with the radio. He took Beth right home. "See you in school, Laurey," he said as the car came to a stop in front of her house.

All his explanations still hadn't taken the hurt away. She hadn't accepted his invitation to watch him dance with everyone but her. To her, that wasn't very special.

"Sure. See you," she said reaching for the door handle.

"Come here." Sandy grinned and pulled her toward him. He kissed her. His kiss wasn't anything like she'd imagined. It was rough and demanding. Under the mint she detected something stronger.

Beth pulled away, opened the car door, and got out. Slamming the door behind her and without a glance back, she hurried up the front walk.

Behind her the car screeched away from the curb.

CHAPTER TWELVE

Waiting and Wondering

Beth tried to concentrate on the play and block Sandy from her mind. But she couldn't separate him from the musical.

She buried herself in her Saturday work at the library, which was always hectic. There were more people in and out, more books to shelve, more cards to sort and file.

Ginny was going to meet Beth for lunch. She hadn't told her friend about the dance. She didn't know if she would or not.

She kept hoping that she'd look up and see Sandy. He'd smile and be embarrassed about the night before. *I'm sorry, Beth*, he'd say. *I was wrong. You're special. You're still my girl, aren't you?*

When she passed the theatre books, she looked for the silent movie book. It was still on the shelf. But there wouldn't be any more envelopes between the pages, no more notes—not then, not ever, Beth was sure. The notes were what made the difference. They were special. If Sandy didn't care, why had he written those notes and put them in the book? That was why she thought she was different from his other girls.

Sandy didn't make sense.

Back at the front desk, a line of people had formed, waiting to check books out. Beth hurried to help Mrs. Forest.

She glanced toward the door as Matt came in. His hair was ruffled from the wind; his face was red.

"Hi, Beth," he said softly, looking over the heads of the two elderly ladies she was helping. "One more day until we know who will play Laurey and Curly."

"Yes, one more," said Beth. Now she wasn't sure she wanted to know.

"What a handsome young man, Beth," said Mrs. Norman, one of the ladies. She nodded her head to her friend. "Don't you think so, Ellenore?"

They should see Sandy, thought Beth, as she stamped their books. But she wondered if Sandy would still want the role of Curly if she was chosen for Laurey. Could they play opposite each other and pretend everything was all right after the way the dance ended? Beth didn't know.

Matt already stood in the check-out line with a book on stage techniques. "Good luck Monday," he said as she stamped the due date in his book.

"Thanks. Same to you."

"See you then," he said and was gone.

Lunchtime finally came. Beth wasn't very hungry, but she still wanted to meet Ginny. Maybe Ginny could help her sort out her thoughts about Sandy.

Beth covered her typewriter and slipped her brown

sweater around her shoulders. At noon there was usually a lull in the library.

"Mrs. Forest, I'm going to lunch now," she said. "I'll be back in an hour. May I bring you something to eat?"

"No, thank you, Beth. I packed a sandwich today. When you return, I'd like you to work on new books. We have a big shipment."

"I'd be glad to," said Beth. She loved working on new books. She always found so many she wanted to read. Working in the library had some advantages. She could check out new books first. There was something delicious about being the first to open a cover, to turn crisp, unwrinkled pages, to smell the binding and fresh ink of a new book.

Ginny waited in the Cadillac in front of the library. Beth ran down the steps. "Want to go to The Wharf or Betty's Burgers?" asked Ginny as Beth opened the car door.

"Betty's will be faster. I have only an hour."

When they turned into Betty's, the lot was overrun with little league baseball players.

"Let's eat in the car," said Ginny. "If we're careful, my father won't mind." She swung the car around the back of the building and behind a green pickup truck in the take-out line.

"Just a hamburger and a small Coke for me," said Beth as the pickup pulled forward.

The girls were next to order. "Two hamburgers—hold the onions—two small Cokes, an order of fries, and a lemon turnover," said Ginny. She turned to Beth. "I'm starved."

"I'd never have guessed."

Ginny grinned.

In a few minutes the blue-uniformed girl handed a white bag through the car window. Ginny passed the bag to Beth, then pulled the car into an end parking space. Carefully the girls arranged their Cokes and hamburgers on the glove compartment door. They put the fries and Ginny's turnover on the front dash.

"I was watching you on the way over here. What a sad face, Beth. You seem so depressed. What's wrong?" asked Ginny between sips of Coke.

"Everything." Beth unwrapped her hamburger but didn't start to eat.

"What's everything?"

Beth told Ginny about the skating rink and then the dance.

"That rat! You should have asked Matt to take you home both times. Beth Winston, if I were you, I'd never say a word to Sandy Grange again. I wouldn't even say goodbye. I wouldn't say anything."

"My rational part agrees," said Beth with a sigh. "But—Oh, Ginny, I don't know. He couldn't have meant to hurt me. There are the notes. Maybe I should have gone after him at the dance. Maybe I shouldn't have danced with Matt. And I know I embarrassed him at the skating rink. I embarrassed myself."

Ginny shook her head and put her Coke down. "Your only fault, Beth, is that you're too nice. Stop trying to put the blame on yourself. I hate to say 'I told you so,' but Sandy isn't for you, Beth. I'm afraid he's as rotten as he seems."

"But, Ginny, he just can't be. When I'm with him, it's like I'm somebody. Everyone looks to see who's with Sandy."

"I won't argue with you about that, Beth. Ask

yourself why they look though. Beth, you're somebody all by yourself, don't you know that? Please believe me, if he never calls you or never asks you out again, good riddance; count yourself lucky. Sandy is selfish trouble."

Beth looked out the side window. She didn't want to listen to Ginny. "There's still the play to consider," she said.

"What about the play?"

"Sandy and I could be starring opposite each other."

"I doubt it," said Ginny, waving a french fry at Beth. "Sandy doesn't deserve the lead. Matt does and you do, but not Sandy."

"You really don't like him." Beth could hear the dislike in her friend's voice. There was no question of jealousy, she knew that now.

"No. I really don't." Ginny took two more french fries. "Let's talk about something else."

"We don't have much time. I have to be back at the library in fifteen minutes. And I've been talking and not eating."

"Have a few french fries."

"No thanks."

The hamburger and Coke churned in Beth's stomach. Was Ginny right about Sandy? Beth didn't want to think about it anymore. In her heart she knew that if Sandy asked her out again, she probably wouldn't say no. Somehow she couldn't believe he was as bad as Ginny said.

The rest of the weekend flew by. Talking to Ginny hadn't helped at all. Beth still felt as mixed up as ever.

Maybe when I hear the announcement for the play, I'll know my true feelings, she decided.

The atmosphere in drama class was tense. Everyone waited anxiously to hear who had been chosen for the leads. No one could get a clue from Mr. Jordan's face. He knew his craft well. He acted as if it were an ordinary school day.

When he looked up from his papers, he had only to clear his throat. There was instant silence. "The auditions are complete. The female lead, Laurey, will be played by . . ." Mr. Jordan paused to build suspense, "by Beth Winston."

Clapping. Congratulations. Beth was speechless. When dreams come true, how are you supposed to act? What are you supposed to say? she wondered.

"The male lead . . ." said Mr. Jordan.

Everyone was quiet again. Beth glanced at Sandy. He was smiling. Matt was sitting too far back in the room for Beth to see him without turning and being obvious.

". . . hasn't been decided yet. I'd like both Sandy and Matt to stay after class to run through a few more lines and a song. Beth, I want to see you after class also."

"Aww," went the class.

After announcing the rest of the cast, Mr. Jordan said, "Now, let's work on the music."

Everyone sang, but Beth's voice seemed to soar over the others. Her heart kept time to the music.

I am Laurey, she thought, and could hardly believe the part was actually hers.

When class was over, Beth was the center of

attention. "I told you the part would be yours."

Ginny hugged her. "I'm so happy for you, Beth. And I'll work at the library the days you can't, if it's all right with Mrs. Forest. So don't worry about your job."

"Oh, Ginny, you really would do that for me? You're a real friend." Beth hugged her back, and they both laughed.

"I'll save you a seat in the cafeteria," said Ginny. "Try not to be too long."

"I'll hurry," called Beth as Ginny headed for the door.

"Congratulations, Beth," said Matt coming up behind her.

Beth turned. "Thanks, Matt."

He took her hand and squeezed it gently. "Wish I didn't have to wait on the other decision."

"You'll probably know by tomorrow," she said and could imagine how he felt.

"I don't know. Mr. Jordan says by Friday." Matt sat on one of the desks and studied his script.

Beth looked around for Sandy. He was talking with Mr. Jordan. She waited for them to finish.

Finally Sandy turned away from the teacher. He came over to Beth. "Well, you got *your* part," he said.

"Yes, I can't believe it." Beth looked over at Mr. Jordan.

He smiled. "You'll believe it, Beth," he called. Mr. Jordan had heard her. "Remember, I want to see you for a minute as soon as the rest of this room clears out." He went to the back of the room to speed a few stragglers out the door.

"Beth? Would you like to go to a party with me?" Sandy was looking over a copy of his script when he asked. He looked up. His face was serious.

Beth was surprised. She wondered if her feelings showed on her face. An invitation to go anyplace with Sandy was the last thing she expected on that day. "When?"

"Wednesday night."

"That's a school night."

"Yeah. I guess I forgot. Your parents probably won't let you go." Sandy sighed and shrugged.

"No. I mean, yes, I'd like to go." Beth accepted quickly, then wondered why. Sandy was right. Her parents wouldn't like her going out in the middle of the week. And now with the play to rehearse, plus working out a schedule with Ginny, Mrs. Forest, and Mr. Jordan, she'd be extra busy. But she didn't take back her acceptance.

"The party is at Eddie MacIntyre's place at Paradise Cove. I'll pick you up at eight." Sandy grinned at her.

Now Beth really wondered if she should have accepted Sandy's invitation. Eddie MacIntyre lived in a mansion. Beth had never been to a party on the beach. She didn't know how to act or what to wear.

"Beth?" Mr. Jordan called.

Everyone but Matt and Sandy had gone. They sat on opposite sides of the room, both engrossed in their scripts.

"I understand you work at the library after school," said Mr. Jordan. "Ask if you can work later on Tuesdays, Thursdays, and Saturdays. On Monday, Wednesday, and Friday we'll rehearse after school, plus lunch hour every day. With those days and class time, I think we'll get enough rehearsal. Then we'll have spring vacation, but near the end we'll need some weekend rehearsals. You might warn Mrs. Forest when that time comes."

"My friend, Ginny, said she'd fill in at the library for me. She's working on props so I hope she'll be able to do both."

"No problem for either of you," said Mr. Jordan. "That's good. You'll make a wonderful Laurey. I'm counting on you, Beth."

"I won't let you down, Mr. Jordan. Thanks."

"I know you won't, Beth. That's all for now. You may go to lunch. Matt, Sandy, ready? Do you have your scripts? Sorry to put you both through this. The decision is a tough one. I want to be fair."

Beth slipped out the door and hurried toward the cafeteria. Her face hurt from smiling so much, but she couldn't help herself. Her mouth kept spreading out into a wide, turned-up line. The only way to change it was to sing. She burst into the theme song from the play.

Beth tried to keep her voice low in the almost empty hall, but she was so happy, she was certain to explode if she didn't sing something.

CHAPTER THIRTEEN

Oh, What a Beautiful Day

"Mom? Dad? Anybody home?"

"In the study, Beth. What's wrong?" Her mother peered out from the study. Concern showed on her face.

"Relax. Nothing's wrong," said Beth, closing the front door. She skipped down the hall and tossed her sweater so it landed on the banister.

"Aren't you home early today?"

"Uh-huh." Beth smiled at her mother, then laughed.

Her mother looked at Beth as if she didn't recognize her own daughter.

"I got it!" yelled Beth.

"Got it?" Her mother sounded as if she thought Beth was talking about the measles. "Got what?"

"The lead—the part of Laurey in *Oklahoma!* Mr. Jordan announced his decision today."

"Beth! That's marvelous!" Her mother threw her arms around Beth.

"What's going on out here? Sounds like the

Fourth of July.'' Her father came to the study door. He peered over the top of his reading glasses, balanced on the very end of his nose.

''Beth got the lead role in *Oklahoma!*, David.'' Her mother sounded as excited as Beth felt.

''The lead role! This calls for a celebration. Shall we send out for Chinese food?''

''Oh, could we? It's been ages since we've done that.'' Beth jumped up and down like a five-year-old, but she didn't care.

''The budget will adjust to a small celebration for a big event,'' said her father. ''We're proud and pleased, Beth.''

''Thanks, Dad,'' she said, suddenly shy with her own father.

They were like a family again. It was the way they used to be before—before Sandy.

Her father withdrew into the study again and left Beth and her mother to choose the menu for the celebration dinner.

While they ate chop suey and egg rolls by candlelight, Beth tried to think of a good way to bring up Wednesday night's party. There wasn't one. She knew if she mentioned the party or Sandy, their wonderful dinner would be spoiled. So she put it off. I'll tell them later or in the morning, she decided.

They sipped pale oriental tea and nibbled sweet almond cookies. Everyone saved his fortune cookie for last.

What will mine say? Will I fall in love with a handsome stranger? If mine says that, I hope it also tells me how I'll know it's love, thought Beth, looking at the crisp, pale shell on the edge of her plate.

"Fortune time," said her father. His cookie fortune said, HARD WORK BRINGS MUCH SUCCESS.

Her mother's said: LIFE'S COMPANION WILL GRANT SECRET WISHES TONIGHT. That brought a smile to Beth's father's face.

Beth bit into the brittle cookie. She pulled out the thin paper strip. "Mine says: BEWARE OF WOLF IN SHEEP'S CLOTHING. Not very original." She passed the fortune around so her parents could read it too. She wished her fortune had been romantic.

"But good advice nevertheless," said her father lightly.

Beth guessed what and whom he meant. "I'd better hurry with the dishes and work on my lines," she said quickly.

"There aren't many, so I'll do the dishes tonight," said her father. "Part of the star treatment."

"Thanks." Beth gave each of her parents a quick kiss, then hurried upstairs.

Before she started her homework, she decided to write about her day in her diary. After taking the little book from her desk, she also took out and read her two S. W. A. K. notes. Would Sandy ever admit he wrote them? she wondered. Folding the notes, she returned them to their safe, secret place, then she turned to that day's page in her diary. She uncapped her pen and began.

Dear Diary,

Today I got the part of Laurey in *Oklahoma!* I still don't know who will play Curly though. Mr. Jordan says he'll decide by Friday. Will it be Sandy or Matt? I wish I knew.

We had a celebration dinner at home tonight—Chinese food, my favorite. It was super. I felt like part of the family again instead of an army of one on the opposite side of a battlefield.

Ginny says she'll substitute at the library for me when I can't work. Mrs. Forest agreed. She's wonderful. She promised to tell me about her high school play. Sometimes I forget that older people once went to school and had dreams too.

One problem solved. Now I have to decide what to wear Wednesday night. I haven't told Ginny about the party. She'd just get upset and lecture me. I haven't told my parents yet either. They'll do the same, I'm afraid.

I didn't think I'd ever want to go out with Sandy again, but when he asked me to the party I was like Ado Annie Carnes in the play. I couldn't say no.

I have to go through my closet now to see if I have something nice to wear to the party. What do you wear to a mansion anyway?

Love,

B. W.

Beth slipped her diary back in the secret place. She was afraid to tell her parents about Wednesday night, but she knew she couldn't wait too long.

After opening the closet door, she carefully slid

the hangers along the rod. There had to be something—a dress or nice skirt she'd forgotten about. Pants? No. Skirts? Huh-uh. Dresses? Maybe. Navy? Too plain. Yellow? Too summery. Plaid? Too babyish.

Now what will I do? she wondered as she pushed her plaid sun dress aside. I can't ask my mother for a new dress to wear to a party she won't approve of my attending. Beth closed the closet door, then turned down the quilt on her bed and fell on top of the blanket. She wanted the party to be perfect. She had to have a new dress.

Then she remembered she had some money in her dresser drawer. She'd cashed her last paycheck, but she hadn't put any of the money in her savings account that month. She could splurge just once—celebrate her part.

I'll treat me to a new dress, she decided. I'll do it. I'll shop at noon. Play rehearsals won't start until Mr. Jordan makes his announcement about Curly. Tomorrow I'll buy a new dress for the party. Then all I'll have to do is tell my parents, somehow.

As she slipped into her pink pajamas, Beth pictured herself, like Cinderella, dancing with Sandy at the MacIntyre mansion. How many people would be at the party? she wondered. Would there be maids and a butler? Would any of the boys wear suits? Would there be a small orchestra and masses of flowers?

The wind whistled around the upstairs eaves as she snuggled under her covers. Beth could hear the waves pounding the beach. As spring struggled to recapture the coastline, she closed her eyes and drifted into dreamy sleep.

How I wish that there were more clothing stores in Fern Grove, thought Beth, as she hurried along the sidewalk. She didn't have time to take a bus out to the mall on her lunch hour, so she had to find that special dress in town.

Rock music blared from Brenda's Boutique. Inside, the mirrored walls reflected racks of multicolored clothes. Beth found a lime green, crinkly cotton dress on the second rack. It had three-quarter sleeves and a peasant neckline. But when she looked at the price tag, she put the dress back. It was much too expensive. Reluctantly, she left the store.

Farther down the street, at Chic, Cherie, Beth didn't stay long. The saleslady followed her around as if she were afraid Beth would steal everything she touched. Beth could feel the "teenagers-not-welcome" atmosphere.

Time was racing. Beth had only a few minutes before she'd have to start back to school. She had almost passed Dottie's Place when she noticed a dress she liked in the corner of the window. The color was pale robin's egg blue. The bodice had short sleeves, a cape collar, and the skirt was a simple A-line. There was a thin, matching blue belt.

Beth hurried inside the store. "Do you have the blue dress in the window in a size eight?" she asked.

The saleslady looked on her rack. She had only one, and it was Beth's size. "The dressing room is in the back corner, dear," said the woman.

Beth ran. Quickly she slipped the dress over her head. A perfect fit; the color was luscious; and the price was right. She'd even have some money left.

"I'll take this dress," she told the saleslady.

"You've chosen one of my favorites." The woman slipped the dress into a gold-colored bag. "Have a good time, wherever you wear it."

"Thanks. I will," said Beth.

Running back to school, she thought about how well the day was going. She and Sandy would have a good time. Her new dress would bring her good luck.

After work Beth hurried to Arbor's drugstore to buy some new lipgloss and nail polish. Next door to Arbor's was The Play House, the Fern Grove live theatre. A new sign had been posted in front.

Does Mr. Jordan know about this? wondered Beth as she read: OPENING NEXT SATURDAY—THE ALL-TIME FAVORITE OKLAHOMA! TICKETS ON SALE NOW.

Beth decided to splurge. She hurried inside and bought two tickets. She'd invite Sandy to go with her. They could get some tips on how to do their parts. Their parts. For a minute she hesitated. But surely Sandy would be Mr. Jordan's choice, she thought. Not that Matt wasn't good. But, well, Sandy had the experience; he was better looking; he had more personality.

Beth bought the tickets. I can't wait to surprise him, she thought, as she tucked the white envelope containing the two tickets into her purse. I'll tell him Wednesday just before he walks me to the door.

Having a secret was like Christmas in the spring.

Beth couldn't wait.

The air was getting damp, and the sun was setting. Beth had to hurry in and out of the drugstore. She was extra poor, but extra happy, as she hurried up the hill toward home.

CHAPTER FOURTEEN

Another Request

Mom, Dad, there's a party out at Paradise Cove tonight. I'm going with Sandy, but I promise we won't be late.

Mom, Dad, I'm celebrating my part at a party. I'll be home by eleven.

Mom, Dad. . .

There wasn't one good way to tell them about the party.

Beth went up the front steps still trying to decide how to let her parents know without starting another war. Since the Chinese celebration dinner, there had been peace in the house.

Zorro greeted her inside the door. A sense of emptiness surrounded her. The only sounds were the cat's meowing and the tick of the grandfather clock.

Beth headed for the study. She switched the desk lamp on. There was a note on the telephone.

Dear Beth,

We read in this morning's paper that the Indian expert, Dr. Alexander Littlefoot, is in town. We called and were able to get an interview over dinner tonight.

We'll be home around midnight.

Please feed Zorro.

Love,

Mom.

Beth read the note over twice to make sure she hadn't misread any of it. She couldn't believe her luck. Her problem was solved. She kissed the note.

I love Dr. Littlefoot, she thought, even though I've never met or seen him. He would get my award for Keeper of Family Peace.

As she reached to switch off the light, the phone rang. Beth jumped. She answered it.

"Beth?"

The caller was a boy, but Beth wasn't sure if it was Sandy. Sandy had called her only one time, and they hadn't spoken for very long.

"Uh, yes," she said.

"This is Matt—Matt Morrow?"

"Oh, hello, Matt."

"Beth, I was wondering—I mean I know it's a school night and this is the last minute, but I thought maybe—Would you like to go to The Wharf with me for an hour? Sort of a celebration of your part in the play."

Beth sensed what an effort it had been for Matt to call and invite her. He really was a little bit shy.

"Thanks for asking, Matt, but I'm already busy tonight. Maybe another time," she said.

"Oh. I understand. Just thought I'd ask. Well, I'll

see you at school tomorrow then. Goodbye." The phone clicked.

Beth hung up too. She smiled. Matt was a nice guy. She could understand why Ginny kept trying to pair them up. She went slowly up the stairs.

Her dress hung in the closet. Beth took it out and spread it across the quilt on her bed. Would Sandy like it? she wondered.

There was no rush. She could take her time getting ready.

Zorro meowed outside the bedroom door. Beth had forgotten to feed him. She let him in. "Sorry, Z." She scooped him up in her arms. "I'll fix something for both of us."

While Zorro ate in the corner of the kitchen, Beth made a small cheese omelette for herself. Even that seemed filling as she thought about the party.

Hurriedly she washed her dishes, then returned upstairs to get ready.

She ran an almost full tub of water and slid down beneath a blanket of violet-scented bubbles. In the old, claw-footed tub, she could soak almost up to her neck. The warmth of the water soothed some of the tension away. Softly she hummed "The Surrey with the Fringe on Top."

Tonight will be a new beginning with Sandy, she promised herself.

Before she began to shrivel, Beth climbed from the bath and wrapped herself in a large yellow towel. After drying herself, she slipped into her blue-checked robe and fuzzy slippers, then padded back to her bedroom.

The hands on her clock seemed to inch around slowly.

She piled her hair on top of her head. She changed her mind, took it down, and tied it back. Finally she decided simply to brush her hair down, the way she usually wore it.

She sat at her desk and polished her fingernails and toenails with Frosted Appleberry polish.

Finally the time came to put on her dress. She thought it looked even better than when she'd bought it. She slipped the material over her head being careful not to muss her hair too much. A strand of blue and gold beads around her neck and gold, high-heeled sandals on her feet completed her outfit.

Viewing herself in the cheval glass, Beth was pleased with her appearance. Her cheeks glowed pink even without makeup. Her eyes sparkled. Even her hair seemed to behave. Though she appeared serene, her stomach had enough butterflies to lift her off the ground.

She pulled her white shawl from the closet hanger and decided at the last minute to tie a pale blue scarf over her hair. This time she wouldn't arrive at her destination windblown.

Eight-fifteen chimed the clock. A half hour had passed since Beth had come down the stairs. She peeked around the front window curtains as the familiar red sports car screeched to a stop at the curb.

Sandy jumped out and ran up the walk. Beth was surprised to see that he wore blue jeans and a white sweater. Had the party been canceled? she wondered.

The doorbell rang. Beth moved away from the window to answer.

"We're late," said Sandy. "Ready?"

"I am, but . . ." Beth looked at him and then down at her dress. "Maybe I should change. I thought the party was dressy."

"No time. It doesn't matter what you wear. Let's go."

Beth grabbed her purse from the hall chair and made sure the door locked behind her. Sandy was probably right, she thought. There would probably be some people dressed up and some who came casual to the party. Reassuring herself, Beth leaned back against the car seat and listened to the radio.

Paradise Cove was out past the suburbs, an exclusive stretch of private beach where only the wealthiest had their homes.

They passed the mall where the movie theatre and The New Igloo Skating Rink were located. The road wound past the beach on the left. The lights from the groups of homes nestled in the hills to their right were tiny warm beacons in the darkness.

Overhead, clouds moved in to obscure the stars and the moon.

Sandy was quiet during most of the ride.

Beth studied his handsome profile. She realized she knew very little about him, about his family, about his plans for the future. "Do you have any brothers or sisters?" she asked.

"Huh-uh." He turned the radio up.

There were at least a dozen more questions Beth wanted to ask, but she didn't want to shout. She'd ask later or another time, she decided. Maybe on the way home.

The shadowy scenery whooshed by. Beth felt alone as the car sped through the darkness. She shook herself to make the feeling go away and concentrated on the songs playing on the radio. She refused to think of her parents. That would spoil the evening.

The car screeched to a stop at a blinker light, hung like a red eye in the middle of nowhere. Sandy turned left onto a narrow road. He stopped the car at a small white guard shack, barely larger than a telephone booth.

"Hi, Bill," he said as an elderly white-haired man slid the booth window open. "We're going down to Eddie's place."

"Lots of cars through here tonight. Must be another big bash," said the guard.

"Eddie likes to do things in a big way," said Sandy.

"Just tell him it better not be too big or too loud. I can't keep the sheriff out, you know."

Sandy laughed. "You can stall him though," he said.

He stepped on the accelerator, sending a cloud of dirt and gravel spewing out behind the car.

Beth was relieved to hear that the party would be large. She'd feel less self-conscious in a crowd, especially if she was overdressed. She hoped that Sandy and Bill were only teasing about the sheriff, however.

Sandy headed the car downhill, then right along a narrow road. Houses towered along the sand, window to window with their neighbors. Cars that equaled money—a lot of it—lined both sides of the road.

Before they reached the entrance to the MacIntyre mansion, Beth could hear the party. The throb of drums and the whine of electric guitars carried into the night.

At the end of the road were two tall white-stucco pillars topped with entry lights. The iron gates were open. Sandy drove through. Cars were parked everywhere. He squeezed the sports car between a truck and an old Pontiac, then turned off the lights and motor.

"Before we go in, Beth, I want a favor," said Sandy turning to her.

What kind of favor could he want at a party? she wondered.

"Mr. Jordan will be announcing his decision about Curly. I've tried to find out which of us, Matt or myself, he's chosen; but he refuses to say."

"I know he wouldn't tell me either," said Beth. "Besides, drama class is tomorrow. Maybe we'll find out then. You'll probably get the part, Sandy. Don't worry." She was anxious to get inside to see who was there, to see the house.

"I have to get the part, Beth. I've told some of my friends and my parents that it's already mine. You can help me."

"Help you? How?" He had her full attention. "I don't know why you need help now, Sandy. You've already auditioned."

Sandy took a minute to smooth his hair back. He stretched his arms over his head, then brought them down. He smiled at Beth, a little boy smile.

She thought how really charming he was and wondered what kind of a small child he'd been. Did he always get his way with his parents?

"Tomorrow I want you to tell Mr. Jordan that you won't play the part of Laurey unless I'm Curly," he said.

"Tell Mr. Jordan *what?*" Beth couldn't believe what he was asking. She shook her head. "You're not serious? Sandy, I don't have any influence. Mr. Jordan wouldn't care what I say."

"Sure he would."

Beth shook her head again. "No. You're wrong, Sandy. He wouldn't care, and he wouldn't listen."

"You won't do it?" He stopped smiling and stared at her in the dim light from the driveway lamps.

"I can't." She kept her voice soft. "Besides, Sandy," she said optimistically, "you'll get the part, I'm sure."

"Well, I'm not. I heard Morrow audition the other day. He's good."

"I'm sorry, Sandy. You think I have some power that I don't have. Mr. Jordan would give my part to someone else if I said what you want me to say to him."

"That's all you care about—*your* part," Sandy banged his door open, crashing it into the truck next to him.

"That's not true," said Beth, "and you know it."

"Sorry I asked for a favor. Let's go. The party has already started." Sandy walked rapidly.

Beth had trouble keeping up with him on the

gravel drive. She ran and grabbed his arm. He pulled away. She was left to follow behind him through the lighted Spanish arches that framed the entrance to the MacIntyre mansion.

The evening that was going to be so wonderful had started all wrong.

CHAPTER FIFTEEN

The Party

"Sandy, wait. Don't walk so fast."

He didn't seem to hear her. They crossed the brown quarry-tiled porch in single file. Huge tubs of scarlet geraniums were spaced down the long front portico. Even in the darkness, they were visible against the white stucco walls. Beth inhaled their distinctive spicy scent.

One of the two tall, dark-wood, carved entry doors stood open. A shaft of light fanned out onto the outside tile. The music beat loudly. From the house laughter and talking blended with the sound of the band to make a wild cacophony.

Beth followed Sandy through the doorway, finally catching up with him inside. Straight ahead a rock waterfall was centered in a plant-filled atrium. Masses of ferns and other greenery, both standing and hanging, gave the feeling of an intimate rain forest. Beth could imagine how peaceful the area would be without all the people.

A couple, kids she'd seen at school, were sitting in

one corner of the atrium taking advantage of the atmosphere.

The band stopped playing as she and Sandy turned toward the room on the left. He hadn't looked at her since they'd left the car. Now he seemed to be pouting, she thought, feeling a thread of irritation unravel some of her earlier excitement.

Sandy seemed to scan the crowd. Two steps down, the large living room was packed with partying kids. Beth couldn't see anyone who looked older than twenty.

A polished, Spanish-tile floor spread across the room to a curved fireplace. A gas log flickered in its cavelike interior. Intricate woven and embroidered wall hangings decorated some of the stark white walls.

Every piece of beige, linen-covered furniture seemed to be occupied with one or more couples. There were a lot of kids Beth didn't know.

"Hey, Sandy, wondered if you'd make it." Eddie waved from the far corner of the room. He climbed over the back of a chair, leaped over a table, then came toward them.

"There's food and things to drink, all kinds, in the other room," he said. "Help yourselves. Don't know what else is here, but you'll find out. Have a good time. The wardens won't be back for a while, so stay as long as you want." He went back the way he came.

"The wardens?" asked Beth.

"His parents," said Sandy sarcastically. "Eddie gets along with them as well as the rest of us do with ours."

Beth didn't like to imagine what her parents would say if they knew she was there.

Someone screamed in the other room, then laughed hysterically. Beth turned in time to see Elsa running from a boy who was trying to shower her with a can of Coke. She headed toward Sandy now. Beth took a step back forgetting that they'd just stepped down two steps. Losing her balance, she sat down hard. Her teeth jarred; her bottom hurt; she felt embarrassed. Quickly she stood up again.

"Elsa, where are you going?" Sandy reached out and grabbed her arm.

"Save me from Roger. He's trying to drown poor little me, Sandy." Elsa giggled and hid behind Sandy.

Sandy swung her out in front of him as Roger caught up with her.

"Who? Me? Drown you, Elsa?" Roger tipped the can of Coke so it trickled down the front of Elsa's blouse. Some of it splattered on the floor and onto Beth's shoes.

"Hey, Sandy, aren't you going to stay at this nice party?" asked Elsa, seeming not to notice what Roger had done to her.

"Sure I am," said Sandy. "Why wouldn't I?" He winked at Roger. "I'll help Elsa clean up," he said.

"Some people have all the luck," said Roger. He tipped the can of Coke back and drank the rest in one swallow, then burped loudly.

"If you're staying at this party, how come she's so dressed up?" asked Elsa, pointing to Beth. "She looks like she's planning to go someplace else." Her voice was baby whiny. She looked up at Sandy, her bottom lip pushed out in a pout.

Sandy glanced over at Beth.

Why hadn't he told her to change before they left? she wondered. She'd asked him about her clothes.

He shrugged as if he hadn't noticed what she was wearing until now.

"I don't know," he said. "Maybe she felt like dressing up. Who cares?"

"Not me," said Elsa. She grinned and put her arms around Sandy's neck, swaying slightly in front of him.

"Sandy." Beth had to yell to get his attention. The band had started playing again.

"What do you want?" He sounded angry.

"Sandy, I want to go home." Beth was scared. She didn't belong at this party.

"You *want* to go home. You *want*." Sandy sneered the words. "Then *go* home. I'm here to have fun." He put his arms around Elsa and pulled her close to him. "Elsa knows how to have fun, don't you, babe?"

Elsa giggled and snuggled close to him.

"Please, Sandy. Take me home, then you can come back. I don't care," said Beth.

Ginny was right. She didn't belong with Sandy's crowd. She wasn't his type, and now she knew she didn't want to be. She had been stupid, blind. She admitted it to herself now, but it could be too late. How she wished she'd accepted Matt's invitation or even stayed home with Zorro.

Sandy turned toward her. She was shocked to see

the look in his eyes. "You think you're so good, so special." His voice was loud enough so that some kids looked their way. "I can't stand a girl who won't make a commitment, Miss Goody-good. Miss Talented. Miss Laurey. Go home if you want. I'm busy." Sandy bent down and whispered to Elsa. She nodded her head.

Beth was humiliated. She stared at the floor. She wanted to run and hide, but she was also angry. Not only with Sandy. Beth was also angry with herself. She'd let Sandy use her to get his grades in math, to become eligible to try out for the play, to maybe even get the lead he wanted so badly. He never cared about me, she thought. That was a fantasy. Sandy cares only about Sandy and about what Sandy wants.

When she looked up again, he was gone—a perfect blend with the rowdy, noisy party crowd. One couple was now standing on a table dancing. Beth turned back toward the entry. She wouldn't stay.

But Paradise Cove was a long way from home. She went in search of a phone. Vaguely she absorbed the beauty of the house but couldn't really appreciate it. She only wanted to leave as soon as possible.

Down the hall she peeked into a library-study where she spotted a phone on the edge of a rosewood desk. Beth tiptoed in. Closing the door behind her to dull the noise, she flipped the wall switch. The room was in startling contrast to the study at her home. The floors were covered with brown plush carpeting. Most of the books were behind polished glass doors. The room was neat down to the letter opener in perfect alignment with the edge of the beige blotter on the desk.

Quickly Beth punched the information number on the push-button phone. "Thank you for using your phone book whenever possible," said a recording. "If you are unable to locate the number you need, please stay on the line and an operator will assist you."

Beth waited patiently.

"Operator. What city, please?"

"Fern Grove."

"Yes, may I help you?"

"I need the number for the Fern Grove Cab Company."

"That number is five, five, five, six, nine, zero, seven. Please mark it down for future reference."

"Thank you," said Beth and hoped she'd never need the number again for a night like this. She hung up and punched in the cab company number. The line was busy. She hung up and waited a few minutes, taking time to look at the shelves of books in the room. Many of them looked new and unread. She guessed they were a collection rather than an enjoyment. Beth lifted the phone receiver and punched in the cab company number a second time.

"Fern Grove Cab."

"Please send a cab to Number Three Paradise Cove Lane."

"I'm sorry, ma'am. Our service area doesn't extend out that far."

"But . . ." The phone line hummed an even tone.

Tears rose behind her eyes as Beth dropped the phone receiver back in place. I can't stay here. I won't stay here, she thought. I'll walk home, if I have to. "That's what I'll do," she said out loud. "I'll walk to the mall. Maybe that's in the Fern Grove Cab Company service area."

Beth picked up her purse from the desk and pulled her shawl close around her shoulders. Quickly she walked back down the hall. At the front door, she stopped and looked across the living room. She didn't see Sandy anywhere. He wouldn't even miss her, she realized as she stepped out onto the front portico. Sandy didn't care at all.

Outside she saw that the fog had drifted in to blow in wisps across the lighted windows of the house. The entry lights, atop the driveway pillars, wore colored halos.

Beth hurried toward the road. The crash of waves on the beach and the crunch of gravel under her feet seemed louder in the fog. Behind her she could still hear the raucous sounds of Eddie's party. The road ahead was dark.

Beth shivered and pulled her shawl closer. She was tempted to turn back as her imagination conjured up horrifying scenes from every scary book she'd ever read, from every frightening movie she'd ever seen. If she'd been wearing flat shoes, she'd have run.

Beth knew what a real sense of relief was when she saw the guard shack ahead. She was cold and out of breath when she finally reached it.

Bill slid the shack window back and called to her, "You have car trouble, miss?"

His kindness pulled the stopper on her tears.

"Hey, hey, can't be that bad." He opened the

door and came out. He moved slowly with a slight limp. He didn't stand quite straight, but bent slightly forward as if a strong wind were pushing him. In the glare from the roof lights, his face looked wrinkled, and his eyes were deep blue and sympathetic.

"The par—party," she said, sniffling.

"Another one, eh," he said shaking his head. "Never fails. Every time Mr. and Mrs. MacIntyre leave town, that kid has a bash. Don't know why they don't have someone responsible stay with him or just leave him at the sheriff's station. More often than not, that's where he ends up." He motioned toward the small shack. "Come in out of the fog, miss," he said.

With the huge window that fronted the closet-sized shack, plus the lack of room inside, Beth figured she was as safe there, if not safer, than she was anyplace. She accepted his hospitality and stepped inside.

"Why don't you call your folks?" said Bill.

"They aren't home."

"Umm." He nodded his head. "Got a friend?"

"Friend?"

"Girlfriend? Boyfriend? Someone who will drive out to get you."

"Ginny," said Beth. "Maybe—"

"You know the number," he said. "There's the phone."

Beth wiped her tears on the edge of her shawl, then dialed Ginny's number. She wondered why she hadn't thought to call her earlier.

Mrs. Rose answered the phone.

"Is Ginny home?" asked Beth.

"You sound strange, Beth. Are you sick?" asked Mrs. Rose.

"I'm not sick. May I speak with Ginny?"

"Of course, dear. Just one moment."

Beth took a deep breath. She looked over at Bill. He was playing a game of solitaire on the ledge inside the window.

Ginny picked up the receiver on the other end. Beth heard the click as Mrs. Rose hung up the other phone. "Hi, Beth. Your phone sounds fuzzy, like you're far away. Can you hear the noise? Must be the fog in the lines."

"Oh, Ginny. I am far away." The tears started again.

"What's wrong? What happened, Beth?"

"I'm out at Paradise Cove. Sandy brought me to a party. I want to come home, but I don't have a ride."

"What's the address?"

"I walked to the little guard shack at the cove entrance."

"Stay there. I'll be right out."

"Ginny?"

"What?"

"Thanks."

"You'd do the same for me."

"I hope I never have to." Beth hung up the phone. She turned to Bill. "Thank you," she said.

"I love rescuing damsels in distress," he said.

"You are a real knight in shining armor." Beth was able to smile a little again. "Even if your castle is small," she added.

Bill chuckled.

While she waited, they played gin rummy on the window ledge. Bill won every time, but Beth didn't mind a bit.

The sight of the Rose's white Cadillac pulling up next to the guard shack was welcome. Beth thanked Bill again for his help and hospitality and went to meet Ginny.

"Do you want to come to my house?" asked her friend as she turned the car around. "Or do you want to go home?"

"Home, please," said Beth. She rested her head on the back of the seat and closed her eyes, trying to block out the first half of the evening.

"Is it finally over?"

Beth opened her eyes and turned to her friend. "What?"

"Your infatuation with Sandy?" Ginny turned the car onto the highway, and they started back toward central Fern Grove.

"Infatuation." Beth sighed. "I think it was worse, Ginny. More like obsession. Yes, it's over for good, forever."

"Good," said Ginny. "I'm sorry you got hurt, Beth."

"It's my own fault, Ginny." Beth was surprised that she no longer felt like crying. In fact, she felt suddenly released, free. "Next time I'll know that I can't judge a boy by his looks or, as Mrs. Forest would say, a book by its cover."

"Not all handsome boys are like Sandy, though," said Ginny.

"I know that," said Beth. "But his looks were all

that I saw. Appearances were everything; how we looked together; who was impressed. I guess I was as bad as Sandy in a way. I wanted top status with a group from him. He wanted the lead in the play from me."

"You've got first-class status. You just don't know it," said Ginny.

"Thanks," said Beth. "That seems to be all I can say to you tonight."

"That's enough." They passed the library and school. Then Ginny dropped Beth at home. "I'll see you tomorrow," she said.

Beth waved as the Cadillac pulled away, then hurried to get inside. She was glad her parents were still out. She didn't want to explain the evening to them. She only wanted to forget it completely.

As she opened her purse for the house key, she saw the small white envelope. She'd forgotten about the tickets. She'd never told Sandy about them. Oh, well, she thought, maybe Ginny will go with me.

One thing Beth knew for certain. If Sandy got the part of Curly, she would withdraw. She'd choke singing "People Will Say We're in Love."

In her room she hung her dress at the far end of the rod in her closet. Will I ever wear it anywhere again? she wondered.

Before climbing into bed, Beth knew she should write in her diary. She should record the death of her feelings for Sandy as she'd recorded their birth. But she knew that in the secret place where she kept her diary, she also kept the S. W. A. K. notes. The realization that the words written in them must have been a huge joke, a joke she took so very seriously, hurt too much yet. She didn't want to see them. Maybe tomorrow night she could make a late entry and tear up the notes. But not yet. She had no emotional strength left.

Beth crawled into bed and pulled the covers up to her chin. Zorro jumped to the foot of the bed and curled up contentedly next to her feet.

As sleep started to settle over her, Beth couldn't help but wonder when Sandy would notice that she'd left the party. She wondered if he would notice at all.

CHAPTER SIXTEEN

The Final Note

Beth dragged her feet as she walked down the hill to school. Her anger had cooled, but nervousness took its place. Would Sandy say anything about the night before? she wondered. Would he and his friends laugh because she'd left the party?

The fog still hung on the water, a gray day to match her gray mood. She had felt so brave and right to leave the party the night before, but in the morning she was afraid. No one liked to be laughed at or teased, and she had a feeling that Sandy and his group were very good at both.

"Beth, wait for me."

She turned to see Ginny running down the hill. Her dark hair streamed out behind her. She was out of breath when she caught up. "Don't worry about today," she said, puffing. "Remember how rotten Sandy has been, and you'll make it through. Knowing him, I bet he ignores you."

"I'm not so sure," said Beth. "I doubt many girls walk out on him. What if he wants to get even?"

"He won't let anyone know that you mattered that much. Believe me, he'll pretend he doesn't even know you."

"I didn't matter that much," said Beth, being honest with herself and Ginny.

Ginny touched Beth's arm and smiled. They continued toward school.

Ginny sounded so certain about Sandy and how he'd react, Beth's fears receded slightly.

In the hall before the bell rang, she watched for Sandy or the others who were at the party. Beth saw a few of his friends, but they didn't seem to see her. Ginny must be right, she thought, as she took her morning books from the locker.

"I have to get to class early," said Ginny. "We have a test this morning. See you in drama."

"All right. Either today or tomorrow will be announcement day again," said Beth.

"Beth, what will you do if Sandy gets the role?"

Beth had wondered how long it would be before Ginny asked her that question.

"I'll back out of playing Laurey. I can't play opposite him now."

"He'd better not be Curly then," said Ginny.

"I can't decide for Mr. Jordan. I have to accept his choice."

The thought that she might lose the part she had wanted so badly depressed Beth. Her mind struggled with ways in which she could be Laurey if she was matched with Sandy. I'm not that good an actress, she thought. I don't think it's possible.

A fresh dose of anger surged through her. Sure she was partly to blame, but Sandy may have ruined her whole year with his selfishness. She detested him with the same intensity that not too long before she'd loved him with.

"Where's Elsa today?"

The question, coming from somewhere in the crowd milling about in the hall, made Beth turn to see who had asked it. It was Pam. She walked with Sandy and some of the other members from his group.

"She can't get out of bed," said Eddie and laughed. "Isn't that right, Sandy? She can't get out of bed?"

Beth turned back to her locker. Poor Elsa, she thought. She was also in love with Sandy, Beth knew now. She felt sorry for Elsa.

Beth looked over her shoulder as the group passed. Sandy stared directly at her, but it was as if he were looking at a wall. His face was blank. It was obvious that Beth was never important to him the way he was to her. He never even thanked me for my help in algebra, she realized as she closed the locker door and headed for her own class.

Walking down the hall, Beth was disgusted with herself for wasting so much time on Sandy. Yet, deep inside, there was an ache. She wasn't sure if it was her heart or her pride which hurt most, but she knew that she'd never be the same girl who found that first S. W. A. K. note in the library.

Beth started up the stairs to the second floor. How like Sandy, she thought, never to admit that he wrote the notes or put them in the book. In many ways she wished she were a vengeful person. But she wasn't.

* * *

All day Beth had managed to stay angry with herself and with Sandy. As she crossed to the library that afternoon she knew that it would be the most painful part of her day.

Inside, she hurried to get the book cart. I must keep busy, she thought, and began to shelve books.

A while later as she pushed the cart down the aisle, she approached the theatre section. Beth had saved that section for last. As she reached the theatre shelves, the hurt inside grew too large to contain. She tasted the salt of the tears that rolled freely down her cheeks. She rested her head against the shelf edge and cried silently. How much those notes meant to her!

Her only consolation was that Sandy wasn't in the library, witness to her upset. Beth took a deep breath and stretched upward, trying to keep on working; but the tears blurred her eyes so she couldn't read the book titles.

Her purse was in the office so she had no tissue. Like a small child, she wiped her eyes with the backs of her hands and pressed fists against her closed lids to hold back the tears.

"Beth, what's wrong? Are you sick? May I help?"

Startled, she opened her eyes.

Matt stood next to her.

She sniffled and turned toward the shelves, but he came around to the other side, so that Beth was forced to look at him.

Concern showed in his eyes. "Here," he said, handing her a neatly pressed white handkerchief.

Beth blotted her face and eyes. "Thanks," she

mumbled. She stared at the floor, embarrassed at having been found in a state of flooding tears. She didn't know what to say to Matt. She couldn't look at him.

Near his feet she saw a white envelope. Glad to have something to do, she bent and picked it up.

Matt reached out to take it from her. "I must have dropped that when I gave you the handkerchief," he said, reaching out to take the envelope.

Beth turned it over. At that moment her heart and tears stopped together. The neat printing on the envelope was familiar. Her name, as before. She was certain surprise showed on her face as she looked up at Matt.

"Forget about the notes," he muttered, taking the envelope from her hand. His face was crimson. "That was a dumb thing for me to do. I got the idea from my kid sister, who was writing to a boy she met at camp last year. On her envelopes she always puts . . ." He stopped. "I'm sorry, Beth," he said. "I know you're going with Sandy. It's just that I wanted to know you better, and I'm not very good at talking to girls."

"You're wrong," said Beth.

"Wrong?"

"I am not going with Sandy. I am never going anywhere with Sandy again. And, you've spoken to me quite often. I haven't noticed that you had any problem."

"That was general talking about the play and stuff, not serious talking or asking you out." Matt's face was still red. "I'd better get back to studying," he said. "I hope you're feeling better."

"I'm feeling much better," said Beth. She smiled at him. "Thanks."

Beth tucked his handkerchief in her skirt pocket and shelved the books for that section, then she went back to reload the cart. She started her next group of books, pushing her cart through the fiction aisles. She felt as if a weight had been lifted from her.

Matt had put the notes in the book. Matt was the poetic one. He wanted to know her better. And *he* meant what he wrote. The notes weren't a joke.

Beth smiled as she remembered their meetings at her locker, the show, the rink, the dance. Had he been there because somehow he knew she'd be there too? Sometime, maybe, she'd ask him.

As she turned the cart at the end of the aisle, Beth looked over at the study tables. Matt's head was bent over his books. Beth wondered if he was studying, or was he thinking about her as she was thinking about him. He looked up just then as if aware of her thoughts.

A sense of serenity, a glow of happiness pushed away the gnawing hurt that had been aching inside her.

Wait until I tell Ginny it was Matt who wrote the notes. She'll be so surprised, thought Beth. Or will she? Ginny always did say he liked me. This time Beth didn't mind remembering her friend's words.

CHAPTER SEVENTEEN

The Announcement

The sky was still gray as Beth got ready to leave the library. She looked out the front window. A fine mist hung in the air, enough to make the trees and bushes drip—changeable spring weather.

"I'll drive you home, if you want." Matt stood next to her, and they looked outside together.

"If it's not out of your way."

"It's not," said Matt. "Where do you live?" He grinned.

Beth laughed. "Just up the hill. I can walk."

"No. My car is right outside."

Beth said good night to Mrs. Forest.

Matt took her books and opened the library door for her. In the lot he led her to an old white Pontiac. "Not beautiful, but fairly reliable, with emphasis on the 'fairly,' " said Matt.

The interior of the car was blue and smelled of mild lemon and spice. The scent brought back pleasant memories to Beth.

Matt ran to the driver's side and climbed in. He

started the car and backed it up carefully. "Listen," he said, slipping a cassette into the tape player under the dash.

Familiar music from *Oklahoma!* filled the car.

"Helped me practice expression," said Matt as he turned left onto the street.

Beth sang along, and Matt joined in. "I live just over the top of the hill," she said. "There." She pointed to her house.

Matt signaled and turned the car into the driveway. He clicked the tape player to off.

"Thanks for the ride," said Beth, opening the passenger door, "and good luck tomorrow."

"You're welcome, and I'll need it," said Matt. "See you in the morning. And, Beth, I am sorry about those notes."

Beth looked at him. "I'm not," she said softly. "I saved them." She slammed the door before he could reply, then ran across the lawn and up the front steps. She turned and waved before opening the front door.

"I'm home," she called, sniffing the spicy aroma of chili cooking.

"Ginny called you," said her mother as Beth poked her head into the study.

"I'll call from the kitchen. Dinner smells good."

"I thought this was a good chili night," said her mother.

"A chilly night for chili," said her father and chuckled at his own joke.

Beth dropped her books on the hall chair and went to the kitchen. She grabbed an apple from the bowl on the counter, then dialed Ginny's number on the phone. "Mom said you called."

"I wondered how you were feeling. Sandy didn't give you trouble, did he?"

"Sandy? Sandy who?"

"Sandy who! Beth, are you all right?"

"I'm fine. Oh, Ginny, you were right. If only I'd listened to you."

"Start from the beginning," said Ginny. "I don't believe what I'm hearing."

Beth told her what had happened in the library. "Matt wrote the notes. I don't know why I never suspected they were from him. He's always in the library."

"Now what will you do?" asked Ginny.

"Nothing. I won't rush into anything again," said Beth, "and somehow I don't think Matt is in a hurry either. He drove me home, Ginny."

"Beth, I'm glad for you. My love life is getting better too. Kevin talked to me today."

"Guess you're going slowly too."

"I don't mind as long as I make progress and get where I'm going," said Ginny.

"Speaking of going, I'd better hang up and set the table," said Beth.

"All right. I'm glad about Matt. See you tomorrow."

Beth hung up. She hummed *Oklahoma!* songs while she set large bowls, silverware, and napkins around the table.

As her parents sat down to dinner, Beth spread her napkin on her lap. She waited until everyone had been served. "I thought I should tell you that I'm not going out with Sandy anymore," she said.

Her father nodded, but didn't comment. Her mother smiled.

She was glad she'd told them and just as glad they hadn't asked why.

After dinner Beth cleared the table. While she washed the dishes, she thought about the next day. Sandy might get the part of Curly. Beth sighed. The happiness she'd felt a short while ago was now tempered by worry about the next day.

Maybe I should warn my parents that I might not have the lead in *Oklahoma!* after all, she thought. No, she decided. I'll wait until Mr. Jordan makes his announcement. Tomorrow is the day.

Announcement day! Sandy stood near the front of the drama room surrounded by his supporters. Beth watched him bask in their admiration.

Matt came in the door as the bell rang. "Good luck," she whispered when he passed her desk.

"Thanks," he said. "I'll need it."

Mr. Jordan kept the class in suspense again—this time for the whole period. Who was his choice? Finally, as bell time neared, Mr. Jordan put the script aside.

"As I mentioned before," he said, pacing back and forth across the front of the room, "the part of Curly has been difficult to cast. Both auditioners are talented. I have decided, however, to give the role to Matthew Morrow. I feel that he and Beth are well matched for the leads."

Beth felt her face burn; she knew she was blushing. Did Mr. Jordan realize what he had just said? she wondered.

Almost everyone clapped for Matt.

Beth turned around. He was blushing also, but he smiled and winked at her when he noticed that she was looking at him.

Across the room, Sandy slouched in his desk. Several members of his group seemed to be urging him to protest the choice. His face reminded Beth of a child denied his own way. He glared and pouted and shook off well-meaning condolences. She realized that he was a child; that his focus on himself—his wants and his needs alone—was immature, even infantile. *What did I ever see in him?* she wondered.

"Sandy," said Mr. Jordan. "Would you play the part of Jud? David has decided he would rather be offstage and work as house manager. Since I hadn't assigned that job to anyone, I've told him he could have the position."

"Jud! That's a crummy part. I don't want to be in the stupid play at all," said Sandy.

The classroom was silent. Then the dismissal bell rang.

Suddenly someone near the back of the room began to hum the song, "Poor Jud is Dead."

"Shut up!" shouted Sandy and stormed out of the room.

"Before you leave," called Mr. Jordan over the sudden buzz of voices that followed Sandy's exit, "the part of Jud Fry is open. Interested auditioners see me now."

Danny McKee was given a push toward the front of the room by a couple of his friends. Danny was a football player.

Beth thought he'd be good in the part if he was as willing as his friends seemed to be. She gathered her books, then looked around for Ginny.

"I told you!" mouthed Ginny, after glancing to see where Matt was.

Beth nodded her head in agreement.

"Beth, Matt, may I see you for a minute, please," said Mr. Jordan, as Danny joined his friends with the news that he had the part.

"Congratulations," said Beth as Matt joined her at the front of the room.

"You're not disappointed?"

"*Not at all.*" Beth emphasized each word so there could be no doubt in his mind.

He actually looked relieved. "I'm glad. I really wanted this part—for more than one reason, Beth." Then his mouth smiled, but his eyes were serious.

Beth felt suddenly shy and could only smile in return.

Mr. Jordan came over to the two of them. "Rehearsal starts Monday noon. If possible, the two of you should do some rehearsing together—especially the duets. Will you try to do that?" he asked.

"We'll do it," said Matt.

Beth nodded.

"Good. This will be hard work from now until June."

"We don't mind," said Matt. "Right?"

"Right," Beth agreed.

"I knew you two were well matched," said Mr. Jordan.

Matt and Beth walked toward the door.

"I'll see you at the library after school," he said. "We'll set up the times for some meetings then. All right?"

"All right. Maybe you can come to my house."

"I'd like that. See you later. I have an English lit test after lunch. Have to study."

Beth watched as he strode down the hall. His shoulders were broad, and he stood a head taller than many of the other boys. His blue sweater was visible for a long while. She watched until she could no longer see him. Beth started toward her locker.

"Hey, over here," Ginny called. "Going to get your lunch?"

"Uh-huh."

"I waited for you. You look like someone hypnotized you and told you not to stop smiling."

"Hmmm?"

"OK. What's going on? If you tell me Sandy apologized, I'll shake you. He doesn't mean it."

"Sandy? Apologize? Never!"

"Then what or who is making you look like a 'smile button'?"

"Oh, Matt is going to come over to my house to rehearse."

"I should have guessed. I'd almost suspect Mr. Jordan of being a matchmaker, but I could never prove it." Ginny spun the locker combination, and Beth took her lunch from inside.

"That thought crossed my mind also," said Beth. "You know, Ginny, you were right about Sandy. I hope you were right about Matt too. I wish I had listened to you."

Ginny staggered and pretended shock. "That's the second time you've admitted that. You've renewed my faith in myself."

Beth laughed. They walked to the cafeteria. She

found an empty table while Ginny went through the line.

"What are you eating today?" asked Beth as Ginny slid a brown plastic tray onto the table.

"Creamed something on cardboard. Tomorrow I will pack my own lunch," she said.

"That's what you always say. Want half of my sandwich?"

"What kind?"

"Ham and cheese with lettuce and mayonnaise."

"I hate mayonnaise." Ginny pushed her lunch around on her plate and ate only a little. "Look at Sandy's table," she said, inclining her head toward one corner of the cafeteria.

Beth tried to look without being obvious. The usually boisterous group looked subdued. Elsa and Jill sat on either side of Sandy, obviously offering comfort.

"One smiles, they all smile. One hurts, they all hurt. Amazing," said Ginny. "If any one of those kids had to make a move on his own, he wouldn't know how."

"It's easy to get caught up with Sandy," said Beth. "He has—I don't know what you'd call it—an attraction of some sort."

"It's called animal magnetism. You aren't thinking of—" began Ginny.

"No. I'm not the worshipping type," said Beth. "I guess that's why Sandy and I didn't go anywhere as a couple. I expected a two-way exchange. He wanted everything one way—his way."

"You know, Beth, I admire you," said Ginny.

"Admire me? Why? I was as blind as the rest of that group, Ginny."

"You admit your mistakes. That's not easy. Sandy has made a lot of kids change to his ways. Look at Pam. She used to be a sweet kid."

"I guess she doesn't have a good friend like you, Ginny, to nag her a little or to talk out her feelings with. I'm lucky."

"Boy, don't we sound like a mutual admiration society," said Ginny. "And while you're valuing my advice, don't let Matt Morrow get away. I think he likes you a lot, and you're a perfect pair."

"Speaking of perfect pairs, I have a pair of tickets for *Oklahoma!* at The Play House. Would you like to go?"

"I'd love to, but I won't."

"Why not?" Beth wondered if something new was wrong.

"Because," said Ginny, "I think you should ask Matt."

"Ask Matt? I couldn't."

"Why not?"

"I just couldn't." Beth thought of how she'd been going to ask Sandy. She didn't want to risk rejection with a second boy.

"Matt isn't like Sandy," said Ginny, seeming to understand Beth's hesitancy. "Think of this as a study date. Mr. Jordan does want you to rehearse together, doesn't he?"

"Yes, but—"

"No buts. Ask him."

Ginny is probably right, thought Beth. "If I ask

him and he says no, you'll have to go with me,'' said Beth.

''Ado Annie would tell you he can't say no.''

''All right. You win.''

They finished their lunches and waited for the afternoon bell to ring. Beth hoped the hours would go by quickly. She couldn't wait to get to the library.

CHAPTER EIGHTEEN

Making Plans

For months Beth had seen Matt at the library. Why, then, did she feel so nervous about seeing him on that day? she wondered. It was as if she were meeting him for the very first time.

Before going to the library, Beth stopped in the girls' bathroom to comb her hair and put on lipgloss.

Elsa was there, making up her eyes. "Too bad you messed up Sandy's chance to get the part he wanted," she said, glaring into the mirror. "I hope your play is a big bust."

For a minute Beth felt herself staring, her mouth hanging open. Then anger at Elsa's nerve and Sandy's cry-baby ways took over. "Sandy had the same chance as anyone else," she said. "Mr. Jordan even offered him another part. Too bad he's such a poor loser. Someone turns his spotlight off, and he falls apart. But I'm sure you'll pick up the pieces and give him appropriate comfort, Elsa. He'll use his loss for all it's worth, won't he?"

Beth didn't wait for her reply. As she slammed out

of the bathroom, she wondered if she had really said all of that to Elsa, one of Sandy's group? I guess so. We were the only two in there.

A month ago she'd have been scared silly to make waves like that. She didn't think she'd even have dared think such thoughts about Sandy, let alone say them.

But that was before you really knew him, Beth, she told herself. And in a way she felt sorry for Sandy and Elsa and all the rest. They were carbon copies, as Ginny said, and didn't dare have opinions or ambitions other than Sandy's.

As Beth walked through the almost empty school halls, it occurred to her that maybe she'd misunderstood what a "dexter" really was. Sure a "dexter" studied hard. But maybe a "dexter" was also someone who thought for himself. Maybe a "dexter" wasn't such a bad thing to be after all. If that's what I am, I no longer care, thought Beth as she pushed the school door open. From now on I'll just be me.

Outside the air was warm. The salty smell of the ocean carried on the breeze.

Beth blushed as she realized she was singing the words to "People Will Say We're In Love."

Slow down, Beth, she cautioned herself as she waited to cross the street. Remember what happened with Sandy.

As she entered the library, Mrs. Forest motioned to her. "Matt Morrow is waiting at his usual table," she said in a low voice. "I'm glad to hear he got the part of Curly in your school play, Beth. You'll do well together."

Mrs. Forest too? Beth wasn't sure that this whole play casting wasn't a matchmaking conspiracy. But if it was, she didn't care.

"Take a few minutes to set up your rehearsal schedule with Matt, then there are some cards to type. Is your friend Ginny still going to work for you?"

"Yes, she is. I'll bring her in on Saturday to show her what to do, Mrs. Forest."

The librarian nodded in agreement and went to check out several patrons waiting at the counter.

Beth put her books in the office and went to the study table where Matt waited.

He took off his glasses as she sat down opposite him. He had the longest eyelashes she'd ever seen. "When do you want me to come over?" he asked.

"Tonight? If you can."

"Tonight will be fine. What time?"

"Seven-thirty."

"Perfect."

"I'll see you then." Beth got up to leave and start her work. She felt very shy with Matt for reasons she didn't know.

"Beth, wait."

She turned back.

"Could I have your phone number again? In case I'm late or something."

"Sure." She jotted the number on a piece of paper.

"Thanks. See you later," he said.

She went back to the desk to type the cards for Mrs. Forest. As she worked, however, she made what seemed like a million mistakes, and she kept glancing over toward the study tables.

This is ridiculous, thought Beth, as she changed her clothes for the third time. Matt is just coming over to study. Slow down, down, down. Why do I have to remind myself so often? Didn't I learn anything from Sandy?

She'd had a bad case of butterflies since she'd left the library that afternoon, and it wasn't from anything she'd eaten, because she couldn't eat either.

Beth changed from her blue sweater to her pink shirt as the door bell rang. "Pink will have to do," she said. Quickly she ran a comb through her hair, then went to her dresser drawer, took out the white envelope, and put it in her back jeans pocket.

"Beth," called her mother.

"I'm coming." Her heart thumped with excitement as she took one last look in the mirror.

When she reached the bottom of the stairs, she stopped. Where was everyone? Neither Matt nor her parents were there. She was sure her mother had called. Was she hearing voices? Did excitement scramble your brain?

Beth went toward the study, then she heard her father laugh. She pushed the door open a crack and peeked in.

Matt and her father had their heads together over some photographs of Indian tribal masks. Her mother sat on the old couch watching them. She looked up as Beth pushed the door wider. "Come in, Beth," she said.

"Hi, Beth," said Matt.

"I guess you've already met my parents."

"Yes," said her father. "Matt tells me that when they graded the road to his house, several Indian artifacts were discovered. His father still has them. I'm going to call and arrange to see them soon."

"You two may use the living room or the kitchen to do your studying," said her mother.

"The kitchen is fine," said Matt. "That's where I study at home."

"Closer to the refrigerator," teased Beth's father.

Matt looked embarrassed, and her father laughed. "I used to do the same thing," he said. "My mother could never understand how I could eat dinner and half an hour later be looking for more to eat." Her father was exceptionally talkative. That was a sure sign that he liked Matt. Beth was relieved.

"Ready?" asked Beth. She couldn't help but contrast Matt's meeting with her parents to Sandy's meeting with them.

"Do you want something to eat?" she asked as she and Matt left the study and went to the kitchen. "There are some raisin cookies."

"Did you make them?" Matt pulled out a chair. As soon as he sat down, Zorro jumped onto his lap. The whole family seemed to like him.

"I'm not sure how to answer that," said Beth. "Will it affect your decision?"

"No. I'll have some whether you made them or not. I was only curious." Matt scratched Zorro's ears.

"I did make them." Beth put a plate of cookies on the table, then poured two glasses of milk. Suddenly she was ravenous.

"Mmm, good," said Matt, reaching for a second cookie.

Beth sat down across from him. She felt the crinkle of the envelope in her back pocket. "You don't have to keep Zorro on your lap," she said while wondering when she should ask Matt about using the tickets.

"He's OK. I like animals. We have a cat and two dogs at home." Matt finished his milk. "Shall we start the rehearsal?" he asked.

Beth nodded and took a deep breath. Now was as good a time as any, she guessed. She pulled the envelope from her pocket, then pushed it across the table. "I have these tickets for next Sunday," she said. "I hope you'll go with me. This might be a good way to learn more about our roles."

Matt opened the envelope. "Tickets for *Oklahoma!* Beth, this is a great idea. I'll take you to dinner before," he said. "OK?"

"OK." He wanted to go! Beth smiled and relaxed.

"Pick you up about six-thirty so we won't have to rush. How about going to Gordon's Galley?"

"We don't have to go anyplace fancy. The Wharf would be fine."

"No. Gordon's Galley is better before the theatre," said Matt. "I insist."

"All right."

Matt smiled and opened his script.

"I'm glad you got the part of Curly, Matt," said Beth.

"I wondered if you would be," he said. "I know I

was." The look in his beautiful eyes made Beth feel wonderful.

"We'd better rehearse," she said, feeling suddenly flustered.

They started at the beginning.

CHAPTER NINETEEN

Oklahoma!—*The Play House*

"May I come in?" Beth's mother poked her head around the bedroom door.

"Sure, Mom." Beth turned one way and then another in front of the mirror. The first time she'd worn the blue dress had been a disaster, but she wouldn't be superstitious and blame a dress for the faults of people.

"You look lovely," said her mother. "Is that a new dress?"

"Fairly new. A treat to myself."

"You deserve it." She stood and studied Beth for a minute. "You need something at the neckline," she said. "I have just the right piece of jewelry." She left the bedroom and moments later returned with a thin, oval silver locket on a fine silver chain. A tiny ring of flowers was engraved on the case. "This was a gift from your father when you were born, Beth," said her mother.

"Oh, Mom. Are you sure you want me to wear this? What if I lose it?"

"You won't lose the locket. I'm sure." Her mother opened the clasp.

Beth lifted her hair so her mother could hook the chain.

"Wear your hair up tonight, honey," she said, "and if you want, borrow my navy shoes."

"But my hair doesn't look right that way," said Beth, putting her hair up so her mother could see.

"You're pulling the sides too tight. Here." Her mother brushed Beth's hair up, putting pins here and there, pulling down small strands near Beth's ears and on the back of her neck.

Looking in the mirror, Beth couldn't believe it was her or her hair. Her mother had made her hair look thick and nice.

"There," said her mother. "You have hair like mine. Sometimes it seems impossible to make our hair look good." She adjusted a strand by Beth's ear, then stepped back.

"Well, you just did the impossible, Mom. Thanks." Beth gave her a hug.

"Your father and I like this young man, Matt, very much." Her mother sat on the edge of Beth's bed while Beth put a comb and a few other necessities in her small purse.

"So do I," said Beth softly.

"Well, he'll be here any minute. Have a good time, honey."

"We will."

"I'll go downstairs now," said her mother, getting up.

Beth tried to think calm as she went to the window and stared out toward the shoreline lights. Her mother hadn't mentioned Sandy, but Beth knew that her parents were glad she wasn't seeing him anymore.

The door bell rang. Beth turned quickly from the window, then made herself slow down. She wanted to make an entrance appropriate for her theatre date.

With her white, lacy shawl over one arm and her head high, Beth slowly descended the stairs.

Matt waited near the bottom of the stairs with Beth's father. "You look great," he said.

"Beautiful," said her father.

Beth almost stopped her descent. Two compliments in two minutes was enough to make any girl dizzy. She felt like a princess.

"We won't be late, Mr. Winston," said Matt as they walked to the front door.

"Enjoy your evening," said her father.

"Yes, have a good time," said her mother. Beth's parents watched in the doorway as she and Matt went down the walk.

The night was warm. Thin streamers of clouds floated across the silver moon. Beth inhaled the scent of the spring night air. She felt marvelous.

Matt opened the passenger door of the car for her, then went around to get in the driver's side. "You have nice parents," he said. "I'd like you to meet my family sometime."

"I'd like that too," said Beth, "especially your sister. How old is she?"

"Lisa is fourteen. She'll be at Meridian High next year."

"I'll watch for her."

"She'll be watching for you too," said Matt. He reached over and took Beth's hand. His hand was big and gentle. "I hope we'll be able to keep in touch, even if I'm away at college next year," he said.

"We will," said Beth. "We have a lot of getting acquainted to do."

"I'm glad we agree," said Matt. He started the car.

Gordon's Galley overlooked the beach. The hostess led them to a table by the windows. Below, in the light thrown from the restaurant windows, jagged lines of foam broke and receded on the sand.

Since they were early diners, the restaurant wasn't crowded yet. The tables were covered with blue cloths and darker blue napkins. The off-white china had a blue line around the edge and a small GG at the top of each plate.

The decor was nautical: ships' wheels, ropes, nets, and other sea-faring equipment. A miniature ship's lantern hung on a wall bracket beside each table and cast romantic shadows.

Beth ordered shrimp, and Matt ordered the fresh catch-of-the-day. They talked of school, films and theatre, and *Oklahoma!* while they waited for their dinners to be served.

"You have such a good voice, Matt," said Beth. "Have you had professional lessons?"

"No, but I sing in the church choir."

"You do? Why didn't you take chorus at school?"

"Because I had to choose between enjoyment and academics to get a scholarship. This year drama was a treat for me," he said. "And I'm glad I made the choice." He reached across the table and touched her hand.

Their dinners came and were delicious. After a lemon tart, coffee, and a long discussion about their pasts and their families, Beth felt as if she'd known Matt forever. When they had finished, Matt helped Beth with her shawl, then they drove to the theatre.

As the curtain rose, Matt reached over and took Beth's hand. Throughout the play she could picture the two of them up on the stage saying the lines, singing the songs, playing the roles of Laurey and Curly.

"This is terrific," said Matt as they joined the rest of the audience in intermission applause. "I feel like I'm ready to put on our production tomorrow."

"All the words are so familiar," said Beth, "but I'm not quite that ready yet."

They got up and walked to the lobby to stretch and wait for the start of act two.

"I hope our play is half as good as this," said Beth.

"Half? It will be as good as this one," said Matt confidently. "Look who the stars are."

"Stardom is going to your head already," teased Beth. "And all this time I thought you were shy."

Matt smiled. "I am shy. It's starring opposite you that has gone to my head."

Beth didn't have an answer to that comment.

The threatre lobby emptied slowly. Everyone was talking about the show and the music. The audience returned to their seats. Act two began.

Beth sympathized with Will and Annie.

Matt gently squeezed her hand as Laurey and Curly kissed and sang "People Will Say We're in Love."

At the final curtain, Beth and Matt stood with the rest of the audience calling for an encore. Finally, when Beth's hands stung from clapping, the theatre began to empty.

Just outside the door, they met Mr. and Mrs. Jordan.

"I see you two are doing your homework," said their teacher. "Glad to have such serious students." He introduced his wife, Elizabeth, who said she'd heard a lot about them.

"Don't tell them I talk out of school," said Mr. Jordan. They all laughed.

Beth and Matt said good night to their teacher and his wife, then started across the lot to the car.

"The music from that show is contagious," said Beth, afraid she would embarrass Matt if she started singing, so she struggled to keep the songs inside.

Matt put his arm around her and began to sing "Surrey With the Fringe on Top."

Beth joined in, and Matt opened the car door while they both continued to sing.

Beth knew they would be wonderful as Laurey and Curly. She peered out the window. The stars winked and flirted against a black sky. The clouds had blown away in the night breeze. She listened as Matt finished the song. He had a wonderful voice. Hearing him sing sent shivers through her.

Matt stopped the car in front of her house.

"I had a wonderful time tonight," said Beth.

"Me too." Matt turned toward her. "You

know," he said softly, "I noticed that there was a lot of kissing in that play. Do you think we should practice a little?"

Beth looked up at him. "We do want to look professional on stage," she said.

Matt bent his head. Beth closed her eyes. His lips were soft and gentle against hers, the way she dreamed a kiss should be.

"I'm not sure that can be improved upon," she whispered as Matt pulled back from her.

"Try again and see," he whispered and kissed her once more.

"You know what?" said Beth as she sat comfortably in his arms.

"Never met him."

"Matt, be serious."

"I am," he said softly. "What?"

"We are going to be great together. Our partnership has just been swaked."

"Been swaked?"

"Uh-huh. S. W. A. K."

"Sealed with a kiss," said Matt. "Maybe those notes weren't such a bad idea after all."

"They were wonderful," said Beth. She leaned her head on his shoulder and wondered if she'd have enough room in her diary for all that had happened that night.

CHAPTER TWENTY

A Marvelous Monday

"Beth, Ginny is here."

"Tell her I'll be right down, Mom." Beth pulled the quilt over her rumpled sheets. She tucked her algebra homework into her notebook, gathered all her books, then hurried downstairs.

"You won't need your sweater. It's warm out," said Ginny. She was wearing blue knickers and a red, white, and blue striped top.

"Which of you is working today?" asked Beth's mother. She stood in the hall, drinking her morning cup of coffee.

Beth's father was already at work in the study.

"I am," said Ginny.

"Practice day for me, Mom." Beth gave her a kiss.

"I'll see you later then, honey." Her mother waved from the porch as Ginny and Beth started down the hill toward school.

"How is everything at the library?" asked Beth. "Are you having any trouble?"

"No. I love it. I never thought the library would be such an interesting place to work."

"Ginny, I have an idea," said Beth. "If you agree, we can talk to Mrs. Forest."

"What's your idea?"

"Even after the play is over, do you want to keep sharing the job?"

"You mean it? I'd love to! But don't you need the money for college, Beth?"

"Maybe not as much money as I thought. Matt has been telling me about some of the scholarships that are available. I have an appointment with Mrs. Crane, my counselor, to get more information and some applications. I think I'll be able to get at least a partial scholarship, Ginny." She didn't add that she wanted time to spend with Matt, because the next year he'd be gone.

"Why didn't you look into scholarships before?"

"I don't know. Guess I was too busy to think about it." Since she'd been going out with Matt, she felt she'd taken much better charge of her life. "But job sharing is settled. All we have to do is talk to Mrs. Forest. Let's do that Saturday, OK?"

"Fine with me," said Ginny.

They turned down the walk to school. Groups of students stood out front and on the steps. African daisies covered the dividers in the student parking lot with their purple and white blooms. Mr. Wiley, the janitor, rode a lawn tractor in front. The air was filled with the aroma of new-mown spring grass. Everyone seemed to have a touch of spring fever. There was a reluctance to go in, to be cooped up in classrooms. The ocean breeze blew sweet and salty.

Beth and Ginny sat on the edge of the planter by the flagpole.

"Summer isn't that far away," said Ginny. "And next year we'll be seniors. I can't believe the time has gone so quickly."

"I know. It's kind of scary," said Beth. "Seems like high school just started, and now it will be over."

"Hi, Ginny. Nice day. Almost beach weather." Kevin ran past them and up the steps into school.

"Looks like you're making progress," said Beth as they got up to follow.

"Slow but sure. He's very shy."

"The shy boys are sometimes the nicest," said Beth.

"You're speaking from experience, of course." Ginny smiled.

"Of course." Beth laughed.

"It looks like 'experience' is waiting at our locker," said Ginny.

Beth looked ahead to see what she meant. Matt was waiting for her.

"I was beginning to wonder if you two were playing hooky," he said as they reached the locker.

"Must be nice to know you're missed, Beth," teased Ginny.

"We thought it was too nice outside to come right in," said Beth, ignoring Ginny's teasing.

"Are you going anywhere Friday after rehearsal?" asked Matt, also ignoring Ginny's comment.

"Home."

"Want to go to The Wharf for a burger?"

"I'd love to."

"Great." Even Matt's eyes seemed to smile. "Don't forget."

"I won't," promised Beth.

"I won't let her," said Ginny.

"See you both in class, then." Matt jogged down the still half-deserted hall, looking back once.

Beth waved, then turned to get ready for class. So much had changed since her recovery from "Sandy-itis"—the way she thought of her previous obsession. Now classes were interesting again. Even her English grades were back up. And her algebra was coming up. She anxiously looked forward to each day and especially to drama class, and not just because of *Oklahoma!*

The play was taking shape nicely. In class they read their lines, working on diction and expression.

After attendance was taken, the prop crew left to work in the art room. Sandy had joined that group. Ginny said he didn't always show up for after-school work, and when he did he goofed off.

Beth no longer cared what Sandy did or didn't do.

That morning the drama class was working on some of the more difficult scenes.

"Matt, Beth, Mary Sue, let's run through the scene where Laurey enters," said Mr. Jordan.

Matt, Beth and Mary Sue, who was Aunt Eller, walked to the front of the classroom.

Shyness left Beth as she became Laurey and Matt became Curly.

The class applauded as Matt held the last note of "Surrey with The Fringe on Top."

"You kids get better every time," said Mr. Jordan. "Beth and Mary Sue, work on your enunciation a little more. And, Matt, don't be afraid to look at the audience once in a while. I know you'd rather look at Beth, but the girls out in the auditorium want to see your face too."

The class laughed.

Matt blushed.

Beth knew how he felt. That was one of the nice parts of their relationship. They seemed to empathize so well. She knew how he'd react—when he was nervous or tense, when he was happy or worried. He seemed to understand her as well, even though they hadn't been going out with each other very long.

The bell rang for lunch. Beth looked for Ginny at the locker.

"Kevin asked me to eat lunch with him," said Ginny, excitedly throwing her books on the locker floor. "Talk to you later."

Beth watched as Ginny hurried down the hall. Kevin is the first boy Ginny has liked this much. I hope this works out for her, she thought.

Remembering how beautiful the weather was outside, Beth decided to eat there. As she pushed the door open, she saw Matt sitting on the lawn, his back against a tree. He had told her he was going to spend the lunch hour studying. He was reading and eating at the same time.

Beth strolled across the lawn and sat down beside him. "Mind if I eat here?" she asked. "I'll be quiet as a mouse."

"I'm glad you came along. It's really too nice to study." Matt closed his book and turned toward

Beth. "I was just thinking about you," he said.

"Good thoughts, I hope."

"Of course. Would you mind if I drove you home after rehearsals?"

"You don't have to, you know."

"I know that," said Matt. "I want to spend more time with you, Beth."

"I'd be glad to ride home with you. Are you still coming tomorrow night and Thursday to rehearse?"

"I'll be there."

"It's too bad this play won't last all summer."

Matt took her hand. "We'll see each other anyway," he said. "I hope you like the beach."

Beth looked up at him. "I like any place you do." Common sense constantly told her to go slowly, but her heart seemed to make its own decisions and put words in her mouth. She didn't take them back.

"The feeling is mutual, Beth. You're very special." Matt bent and kissed her quickly on the forehead.

Beth realized how very much she was beginning to care about him. What she felt for Matt was nothing at all like what she'd felt for Sandy. Real love was deeper, more content, unselfish—a million emotions, all marvelous—which made her feel like shouting and sharing her happiness with the whole world.

After school Beth met Ginny out in front before Ginny went to the library and Beth went to rehearsal.

Ginny was glowing with happiness. "Kevin asked me out this weekend," she said.

"And Matt wants to drive me home after rehearsals."

"Isn't spring wonderful?" asked Ginny.

"Marvelous," agreed Beth.

CHAPTER TWENTY-ONE

The Wharf

"Excellent! What a group!" Mr. Jordan cheered as an audience of one for the cast of *Oklahoma!*

Matt and Beth closed their now-ragged scripts. "I keep thinking I should leave this at home," said Beth, holding up the wrinkled booklet. "I know all the lines. But I have this awful fear that if I don't have the script with me, I'll forget my whole part."

Matt laughed and put a hand on her shoulder. "You sound superstitious. You'll have to let go of your security script eventually."

"I know!" Beth sighed. "I know."

"Don't worry about that now. Are you ready to leave?"

"I'm ready." Beth took Matt's hand, and they hurried through the almost empty school halls.

The Wharf was near the edge of Fern Grove, not too far from Meridian High. The building was old, clad with weathered-wood siding. A huge model ship was displayed in the front window.

Inside, round spool tables were surrounded by

barrel stools. The walls were painted sea blue and decorated with prints of various ships and waterfront scenes.

Rock music blared from speakers in the corners as Matt opened the door and they went inside. Meridian High students filled most of the places. The aroma of french fries and onions made Beth's stomach growl.

"There's a table for two back in the corner," said Matt. He and Beth wound their way past the full tables, stopping occasionally to say hello to someone that one or the other knew.

At the table they shared a menu.

"I'll have a Wharf Superburger and a Coke," said Beth.

A plump, older woman wearing navy slacks, a white middy blouse, and a sailor cap came to the table. "What will you have today, kids?"

"Two Wharf Superburgers, a double order of fries, one Coke, and a glass of milk," said Matt.

When the waitress had gone, he leaned across the table. "Well, Laurey, would you go out in my surrey and take in a movie tomorrow night?"

Beth was about to answer when there was a commotion near the front of the restaurant. She turned around.

Elsa and Sandy had just come in the door.

Elsa pulled away from Sandy. "Leave me alone," she said. "Go for a ride in your precious car." She ran over to a corner table and sat down with several other kids from school.

"Elsa, I said I didn't want to come here. I'm not hungry," said Sandy.

"Tough," she answered. "I am."

Everyone was watching them.

Sandy remained by the door, glaring toward the table where Elsa sat. "I'm going now," he said. "Are you coming, or not?"

"I'm not," shouted Elsa.

Beth felt embarrassed for both of them. She could see other kids whispering across their tables.

Sandy called Elsa an insulting name, then stomped back outside.

"There goes a perfect couple. Too bad," said Matt.

Beth didn't answer. She was watching Elsa. It wasn't easy to turn against Sandy. She wondered if that was the first time they'd argued.

"Two supers, double fries, one Coke, one milk." The waitress put the order on the table. "Anything else, kids?"

"No, that will be all," said Matt.

She left the bill and went to clear a nearby table.

"I feel sorry for Elsa," said Beth as she spread mustard on her hamburger.

"That's what's so nice about you," said Matt as he salted his french fries. "You're sympathetic."

I know how she must feel, thought Beth. "She must be embarrassed," she said.

"You never did give me an answer about the movies," said Matt. He blotted mustard from his mouth.

"I'd love to go," said Beth.

The weekend went by quickly. Back at school on Monday, Beth noticed that Elsa was missing from Sandy's group, both in the halls and at lunch.

In drama class Mr. Jordan postponed rehearsal for the day to hear reports from scenery, publicity, costumes, makeup, and the house manager.

Beth could visualize the entire production coming together as all the committees completed their projects.

"Spring vacation starts this Wednesday," said Mr. Jordan. "Will there be a problem for any of you to meet at my house a couple of mornings to rehearse? This is especially important for those of you with the major roles. Beth, Matt, can you be there?"

"Yes," they said in unison.

"Mary Sue, Joan, Danny?"

They all thought they could make it.

"Good. I won't keep you long, but I want to work on a couple of things. Snacks on the house."

"I love popcorn," said Danny.

"Got it," said Mr. Jordan. "See most of you Wednesday morning, Eighty-four Staghorn Way. That's about a mile and a half north of town. Try to be there by nine."

The bell rang and everyone headed for the hall and the cafeteria.

"I'll pick you up at eight-thirty," said Matt. "Is that all right with you, Beth?"

They stood in the lunch line.

"Fine. You're sure you don't mind? You'll be coming into town, then going back again. I could drive myself."

"I'd like to take you," he said. "We'll go out to lunch afterward."

"Why not go on a picnic? I'll bring the lunch," said Beth.

"At the beach," said Matt. "I know the perfect place for a picnic."

"Sounds great," said Beth. She took a fruit salad, a roll, and a dish of chocolate pudding. "But I should be back to go to work at the library in case Ginny has plans for that day. I don't think the crews have to meet then."

"No problem," said Matt. "But if you find out that Ginny is planning to work, let's spend the whole afternoon together. OK?"

"OK."

The tables were packed. They spotted a couple of vacant places near the center.

Sandy's group sat close by, but Beth was barely aware of them. She gazed at Matt and knew that the afternoons during vacation would never be long enough. Slow didn't work anymore. She was in love with Matt Morrow already.

CHAPTER TWENTY-TWO

Spring Vacation

Matt knocked on the kitchen window.

Beth looked up and smiled. She went to the side door and let him in.

"Mmm. Let's eat lunch now," he said, lifting the lid of the picnic basket on the table. "Chicken, hard-boiled eggs, gingerbread, apples—"

"No snitching," said Beth, closing the top on his hand.

"Cruel, so cruel," said Matt, trying to look wounded and failing.

"How about a cup of coffee and a raisin muffin?" asked Beth's mother.

"Sold, Mrs. Winston." Matt went to the stove and poured his own coffee while Beth took a warm muffin from the oven.

She loved how Matt seemed to fit in at her house.

"How is the book coming?" asked Matt as he sat down at the table.

"Not badly," said Beth's mother. "David is calling now to verify our interviews for this morning."

"We'd better get out of here, or we'll be late," said Beth. "Will I need a sweater?"

"Bring one in case the beach is cold," said Matt. He finished his coffee quickly, rinsed the cup, and put it in the sink. "Thanks for the breakfast, Mrs. Winston."

"You're welcome any time, Matt," said Beth's mother.

The sun was warm, a promise of a beautiful day.

"Ginny said she'd like to keep the same schedule whether we're on vacation or not. So I have all day," said Beth as Matt backed the car out into the street.

"Me too," he said. He slipped a cassette into his tape player, and they listened while Matt drove.

Mr. Jordan's house was in a tract of ranch-style homes just north of central Fern Grove. A mass of ivy geraniums grew in front of the brown wooden home. A split-rail fence edged the yard.

"Some more people are here," called a child's voice.

Beth spotted a little boy, about four, standing behind the front screen. He wore print pajamas, and his red hair was the same shade as Mrs. Jordan's.

"Come in," called Mr. Jordan from inside.

"I'll show you where to go," said the little boy.

Matt opened the door. He and Beth followed their miniature usher down a short hall to a pine-paneled family room. Danny, Joan, and Mary Sue were already there.

"Thanks, Tim," said Mr. Jordan. "We have a few more students coming. Will you watch for them?"

"Sure, Daddy."

"He's cute," said Beth.

"Most of the time," said Mr. Jordan. "May I offer you a glass of juice or an English muffin?"

"Maybe later," said Beth. "I ate before we left."

"Me too," said Matt. "Twice."

A few more of the cast arrived. They sat on an overstuffed green couch and waited for the remaining members. The discussion turned to The Play House production of *Oklahoma!* Many of the kids had gone to see it.

Finally almost everyone was there.

"Tim, time to get dressed," called Mrs. Jordan from the doorway.

"Mommy, I want to watch."

"I need your help making cookies in the kitchen. But you have to put your clothes on first."

"Oh, all right."

"Goodbye, Tim," everyone called.

Beth watched the little boy scamper to his mother. She wondered if Matt had ever been that small. Had he been a cute little boy? What had he looked like? It was hard to picture him as little.

"Beth? Are you with us?"

"Wake up," whispered Matt.

Beth started.

"Welcome back from wherever you were," said Mr. Jordan, not unkindly.

Beth felt herself blush.

"Let's begin. We don't have enough room for the action, so let's concentrate on expression. I want to be able to close my eyes and know from your tone of voice whether you're happy, sad, angry, teasing, etc."

Mr. Jordan sat up on a bar stool. He pointed to Matt. "Begin."

Matt sang the opening song.

When they took a break, Mrs. Jordan treated them to chocolate-chip-pecan cookies, the aroma of which had been torturing them while they baked.

"Does your wife have this week off too?" asked Joan as Mr. Jordan passed the plate of cookies.

"Elizabeth is a career housewife," he said.

"That's right," said Mrs. Jordan as she took the empty plate. "I used to teach junior high school. Maybe someday I'll go back, but right now I'm happy being a wife and mother."

"But don't you get bored?" asked Mary Sue.

Mrs. Jordan smiled and shook her head. "Tim doesn't allow for many boring moments. Parenthood is every bit as challenging as any other career and in many ways a lot harder than I ever expected it to be. I can't leave Tim on a desk and forget about him until the next morning or stop thinking about him over the weekend. Even on the mornings when he's in preschool, I'm aware of where he is, what he's doing, when he'll be home, what he's learning, if he's getting along. I could go on and on."

"I never thought of parenting and housekeeping as work," said Beth. "I guess that's because my mom has always had her writing career."

"Many women can handle two careers, and many women have to. I feel that every woman should have the right to make her own choice without anyone else making her feel guilty. And sometimes it seems to me that those who yell the loudest about homemaking and children being boring don't have a child or keep house. Doing a good job at either one is never easy."

"All right, Liz. Off your soap box," said Mr. Jordan. "We have to get back to *Oklahoma!*"

They went back to rehearsing, finishing up at a little past noon.

"Enough," said Mr. Jordan. "Did I work you too hard?"

"No," chorused everyone.

"Oh. I'll try to do better next time. Any problem with meeting again on Monday, then again Wednesday?"

"I'll have to leave early Wednesday. My grandmother is coming to visit," said Joan.

"That's fine," said Mr. Jordan. "Kids, you're going to be great!"

"Thanks for the cookies, Mrs. Jordan," called Matt as the group started to leave.

"Thanks, thanks," echoed other voices. "Goodbye, Tim," someone called.

The noon sun was hot, a summery day as promised. Matt drove toward Paradise Cove, then past it. He stopped the car along the edge of the highway. The beach below was rocky and deserted.

He took a blanket and the picnic basket from the trunk of the car. Then he and Beth skittered down the rough, weedy path to the sand.

The ocean was calm, the small waves lapping the shore more like the waves of a lake than the tide of the huge Pacific.

"Come on, there's a nice flat rock over there. It will make a perfect table," said Matt.

He spread the blanket beside the rock and Beth set out the lunch. She leaned against the sun-warmed stone. Overhead, sea gulls wheeled, begging for handouts. A slight breeze stirred the salt and fish scents off the ocean.

"I could sit here all day." Beth rested her head back on the rock after eating.

"No rush to leave," said Matt, who sat next to her. "What a good lunch!"

"Thanks," said Beth. She struggled to her feet. "I ate too much. I've got to move whether I want to or not, otherwise I might be here when the tide comes in."

Matt stood up too. He kicked his shoes off. "Let's run," he said.

Beth slipped out of her shoes too. Hand in hand they raced down to the surf line. Splashing and laughing, they jogged through the foam.

"Stop, stop," gasped Beth. "I can't run any farther."

They walked for a while. Beth picked up some small pink shells. Matt disturbed tiny sand crabs, then turned them loose to burrow back into the damp hiding places where he'd found them.

Beth saw a tall rock with natural footholds in the side. She ran across the sand, then climbed to the top where she settled on a ledge, leaning her back against an outcrop. "I am the queen," she called.

"Here comes the king," called Matt, scrambling up after her.

They sat, silent for a while, holding hands and watching the water.

Matt slipped his arm around her. Beth rested her head on his shoulder. "This has been a wonderful afternoon," she said.

"For me too," said Matt. He smoothed her hair back from her eyes where it had been blown by the wind.

Beth stared up at him. She noticed that he had a tiny scar below one eye and that his eyebrows grew in an almost straight line. His eyes were serious as they gazed into hers. He bent his head and kissed her.

"You're very special, Beth," he said. "I love you."

"And I love you too," she answered. Beth rested in the curve of his arm.

They sat that way for a long while.

When they returned to their table rock, Beth cut second helpings of gingerbread for them.

"On Sunday our church choir will be singing at the mall," said Matt. "Will you come and listen?"

"You mean you're singing?"

"Yes. A solo."

"I'd love to come," she said.

The late afternoon sun was warm and golden as she and Matt folded the blanket and closed the picnic basket.

Beth settled herself in the front seat of the Pontiac. Love, she thought, such a small word to describe so many feelings.

CHAPTER TWENTY-THREE

Songs and Sadness

Rows of chairs, already half-full, faced the wooden tiers set up in the center of the mall. According to the signs, there were four church choirs scheduled to sing that day. Matt's choir was first.

Beth sat near the front. She admired the trees in wooden tubs and the masses of potted flowers that transformed the center mall into a spring garden.

The first group mounted the tiers. Matt stood on the left side. The choir was robed in blue and white. Their director stood in front and raised his arms. They began to sing.

Listening to Matt's solo sent shivers down Beth's back. The audience was absolutely silent as they listened.

When the next choir went up to sing, Matt joined her in the audience.

"Thanks for inviting me," she said. "You were terrific. The music was beautiful."

"Thank you," said Matt. "Our choir is like a big family. We all love music."

When all the choirs had finished and Matt had turned in his choir robe, he and Beth went window shopping in the mall.

"Oh, look," said Beth, "there's the pet store. Let's go in."

The store was crowded. A group of children stood around a pen of small chicks. Two flop-earred bunnies in a cage peered out with large sad eyes.

"Oh, Matt, the bunnies are so cute," said Beth as she bent down to peek at them.

"I'd buy one for you, but Zorro wouldn't be too happy."

"I couldn't separate the two of them anyway," said Beth standing up and turning away from the cage. "How I hope someone buys both and loves them."

Matt and Beth left the pet shop and walked past the other store windows.

"Let's go in here for a minute," said Matt. He opened the door of Emmy's Candy Shop.

"May I help you?" asked the lady behind the counter filled with mounds of chocolate goodies.

"One giant-sized bunny, please," said Matt. He put an arm around Beth. "I hope you like chocolate," he said.

"I love it, but—Oh, Matt, I'll never eat all of that," she said, seeing the huge chocolate rabbit.

"I'll help you."

"Uh-huh, I knew you weren't worried about whether or not I'd like it," teased Beth.

"Caught," said Matt, looking guilty.

Beth laughed. She took the bag from the counter. "Thanks," she said.

"You're welcome. Maybe Zorro would like some chocolate rabbit too," said Matt.

"I doubt it. But my dad probably would."

"Good. Share with everyone."

They wandered through the mall for a while.

Beth felt as if the days were only hours, shorter than she wanted them to be. The time she and Matt spent together was never long enough.

The following week, Matt and Beth returned to Mr. Jordan's house to rehearse. They spent another day at the beach, went bicycle riding and ice skating. Beth had a wonderful time.

Then school was back in session. April passed into May.

Beth hurried across the street to the library. "Good afternoon, Mrs. Forest," she said as she slipped behind the counter.

"Hello, Beth. Where's your partner this afternoon?"

"Matt had an eye doctor appointment today. He's getting contact lenses, his parents' graduation gift to him. They wanted him to have them before the play."

"I thought he looked fine with his glasses. A very nice young man, Beth," said Mrs. Forest as she stamped the seven-day magazines.

"Yes, I know." Beth took the returned books from the shelf under the counter and pulled the cards from the file.

She glanced across the library. Sandy was there. Beth wondered what his future would be? Would he outgrow his selfishness? Would he ever care for a girl enough to put her first?

She had no intense feelings left for him, only curiosity and a little pity—also, strangely, a kind of gratitude that she'd learned to differentiate between love and infatuation because of him.

"How is the play coming?" Mrs. Forest was in an unusually talkative mood.

"Very well, Mrs. Forest. I hope you'll come."

"Absolutely. I wouldn't miss it. I remember when I was in high school. One year we performed *Babes In Toyland*. I was a French doll. I wore a short, little blue dress and did my hair in long sausage curls. I stood like this." She stood stiffly, then bent her arms holding her hands up palms facing outward. "That was my entire stage career. But do you know, Beth, I still remember the songs? We had wonderful times rehearsing and performing."

Beth smiled as she pictured Mrs. Forest in her little blue dress and her hair in sausage curls. She still was a little woman and could be a doll even now.

Beth piled the carded books on the cart. She pushed the loaded vehicle around the end of the counter as Jill and Pam came in the entrance. They headed for Sandy's table.

"Have you seen Elsa?" asked Jill loud enough for everyone to hear.

"She's around someplace," said Sandy. He shrugged.

"Why are you being so rotten to her, Sandy?" asked Pam.

"I'm not," said Sandy.

Mrs. Forest came from the front lobby where

she'd been updating the bulletin board. "Beth," she said softly, "there's a young girl sobbing her eyes out in the restroom. She won't tell me if she's sick or what's wrong. I've seen her in the library, though she's never checked out any books. I think she comes in to read the magazines. I know she goes to school with you, Beth. Would you talk with her?"

"Sure, Mrs. Forest. I'll go right away." Beth guessed whom she would find before she pushed open the heavy restroom door.

Elsa stood by the mirror trying to remove the dark smudges caused by her heavy eye makeup running. "What do you want?" she asked sullenly.

"To help you, if you need any. Mrs. Forest was worried about you."

Elsa bit her lip and pushed a tissue to her eyes. Several tears escaped and slid down one cheek. "I don't know what to do," she whispered. "Sandy won't talk to me."

"Oh, Elsa." Beth put a hand on her arm.

"Sandy promised he wouldn't drop me," she sobbed.

"Pam and Jill are in the library looking for you. Do you want me to get them?"

Elsa blew her nose. "No, but thanks, Beth. You're not so bad," she said, "even if Sandy does hate you." The mention of his name started her tears flowing again.

Beth felt helpless. She wanted to get back to work, but hated to leave Elsa alone. She didn't know what more she could say or do.

"He's no big shot anymore, not as far as I'm

concerned.'' The bathroom door banged inward, as Jill and Pam came in. ''Elsa,'' said Jill. She put her arms around the small, blond girl. ''We've been looking all over for you.'' She turned and glared at Beth. ''What are you doing? Gloating?''

''Jill, she's all right. Really,'' said Elsa. ''Thanks, Beth.''

Beth hurried back into the library. Poor Elsa, she thought. She shivered and looked toward the tables. Sandy was gone. His group will never be the same again, she thought.

She pushed the cart of books around the end of the first shelf and headed toward the children's book section.

CHAPTER TWENTY-FOUR

Dress Rehearsal

"Pass the potatoes, please." Matt piled second helpings of everything on his plate. "Great dinner, Mrs. Winston," he said.

"I second that," said Beth's father. "But wait until you taste my apple pie."

"Beth, you aren't eating," said her mother. "Is something wrong?"

"Prerehearsal jitters, I guess," she said. "A touch of stage fright." Beth couldn't believe how Matt was eating and acting as if nothing at all unusual was going to happen the next day.

"It's only a rehearsal," said Matt, "a chance to make all our mistakes before the real thing."

"It seems real enough already," said Beth, pushing her food to the edge of her plate.

"Relax, honey," said her father. "You'll be fine, especially after a good night's sleep. Everyone gets pre-performance jitters."

"Everyone but Matt," said Beth.

"You won't make me feel guilty," said Matt.

"Your mom is a good cook. I won't pass up this kind of meal because of jitters. It's mind over matter. And there's nothing the matter with my mind, if that's what your next comment is." He winked at her.

Beth smiled. They loved to banter words. He was getting to know her well. "We'll see if you're so calm tomorrow," said Beth.

"Anyone for David's apple pie with ice cream and brandy sauce?" asked her mother.

"Me," said Matt, standing up to help clear plates.

"Me, too," said Beth's father.

"Gross," said Beth. "May I be excused to study my lines?"

"Of course," said her mother.

"I'll study with you in a little while," said Matt.

"No rush," said Beth.

"That's right," said her father. "We enjoy Matt's company."

"The feeling is mutual, Mr. Winston," said Matt.

"I'm going upstairs for a few minutes," said Beth. "I'll be back in a little while."

She liked the way her parents had almost adopted Matt. But that didn't change the churning of her stomach, the lump in her throat, the fear of forgetting. Beth ran up the stairs. She really did have a bad case of the jitters and didn't expect them to disappear too easily.

She stood in front of her mirror, combing her hair, wishing she could calm down. She felt jumpy enough to leap out of her own skin.

Picking up the tattered script, she sat on the bed. Her dream of wanting the lead and of hoping that Sandy would star opposite her seemed like years ago rather than only two and a half months.

Sighing, Beth stood up, then went downstairs again.

Everyone helped clear the table, and they all pitched in, a crew of four, to get the dishes done quickly.

"Ready to rehearse now?" asked Beth as Matt folded his dishtowel.

"No," he said. He took her sweater from the back of her kitchen chair and tossed it to her. "We've done enough rehearsing. Let's go for a walk. Then I'll go home, and you can go to bed early so you'll be rested for tomorrow's rehearsal." He opened the side door and ushered Beth out.

"Wow! Is that all, sir?" asked Beth, closing the door behind them.

"One more thing," said Matt.

"What?"

"This." He pulled her close and kissed her. For a minute Beth forgot to be nervous about the play.

They walked slowly, hand in hand, part way down the hill. A mockingbird scolded from a pine tree, disturbed by the hand-holding passersby.

"Warm enough?" asked Matt.

"Uh-huh."

"You aren't really worried about tomorrow, are you?" he asked.

"Yes."

"Oh, Beth. Don't be. We're a team. Together we'll be perfect."

He sounded so confident, Beth felt her nerves relax a little. "But what if I mess up the lines? Forget something? Miss a cue?"

"You won't. I know your cues and part, just like you know mine. And if you did make a mistake, the world wouldn't end. Even great and famous performers make mistakes. So stop worrying, please." He squeezed her hand.

"I guess you're right." Beth sighed. "I just wish my stomach thought so."

"Your dad is right. A good night's sleep will help. We'd better turn back." Matt stopped for a minute in the shadow of an acacia tree. Perfume from the sweet yellow blossoms filled the air. Matt put his arms around her and held her close.

Beth could hear the steady beat of his heart beneath her ear. She felt loved. His confidence seemed to extend like a cape around her.

He bent and kissed the top of her head, then they started back toward her house.

"I can't find my hat. Who took my cowboy hat?"

Backstage at the school auditorium was a chaotic scrambling of drama students looking for costumes, getting made up, and rehearsing last minute songs and lines.

"Keep calm, everyone. This is just dress rehearsal," shouted Mr. Jordan, who seemed anything but calm himself.

"We still have an audience, even if it is the junior high," said Joan.

"Mr. Jordan, will you help us onstage for a minute?" Ginny stood in the doorway of the makeup room looking distressed.

"What's wrong, Ginny?"

"The fence keeps falling over, and Lee, who's

supposed to hold the surrey in place, isn't here yet."

"Have Doug help with the surrey, and I'll take a look at the fence." He hurried out of the room.

Beth peered into the small makeup mirror. Waves of nervousness rolled through her causing her hands to shake. I'll never remember all my lines, she thought. Why did I think this was a good idea? Her jitters seemed worse than they had the night before. She took a deep breath trying to calm herself.

"Five minutes," called Mr. Jordan. "Get ready, Beth."

"Break a leg," called Ginny, as she rushed past the door.

Beth stood up and smoothed her skirt. She went out to wait in the wings for her cue. Matt was already there, waiting for the school orchestra to begin the "Overture." In only a few minutes, he would begin to sing.

There was a hush in the auditorium. The music began.

Junior high students stamped their feet, whistled, clapped, and shouted their approval.

The jitters had completely disappeared. Beth felt as if she could fly. She and Matt, Joan, Danny, Mary Sue, and all the cast joined hands and bowed over and over.

"We were great," said Matt as the curtain closed for the last time.

"Cast party at my house after school," said Mr. Jordan.

"Oh, no. I have to work." Beth wailed.

"No, you don't. I already spoke to Mrs. Forest.

You have the afternoon off. Ginny too," said Mr. Jordan.

"Thanks," said both girls.

Everyone was excited; the play had gone well. All their hard work had paid off.

"All costumes in order. Makeup in the boxes. Scenery stacked for quick reset before you leave," shouted Mr. Jordan. "The opening performance has to be even better than the dress rehearsal."

"Opening and closing," said Mary Sue.

"Any better and The Play House will sign us up," said Joan.

"Don't get too sure of yourselves," warned Mr. Jordan. "We need the same concentrated effort on opening night."

"Look who's getting the jitters now," said Matt.

Mr. Jordan pretended to look around. He had a "who me?" look on his face.

Matt understands people really well, thought Beth as she headed for the dressing room. Sometimes I think he must have ESP.

CHAPTER TWENTY-FIVE

Cast Party

Ginny and Kevin, Danny and Joan, and Matt and Beth crowded into Matt's car. They sang—a musical sardine can moving down the highway.

When they reached the Jordan house, Tim was once more guide and doorman. "Go in the family room. We're having a party," he said.

Matt, Beth, and the group followed his directions. The family room was already filling with talking, laughing students.

"Here they come," called someone. "Let's hear it for the stars."

Everyone clapped and cheered as Beth and Matt entered.

"Just because this is a cast party, don't forget your lines yet," said Mr. Jordan. "The real test is still to come."

"Don't remind us, Mr. Jordan," said Joan. "I'll be scared all over again."

"Pizza anyone?" Mrs. Jordan carried a huge tray

of pizza squares into the family room. The spicy smell of cheese, tomato, and pepperoni made Beth's mouth water.

"I'll take those, honey," said Mr. Jordan. Taking the tray, he passed it around. He held an empty tray in a matter of minutes. Tim was sent to the kitchen to order a refill. Mary Sue followed to help.

"There's plenty to eat," said Mrs. Jordan returning with another pizza tray. "Soft drinks, milk, lemonade at the bar."

"I'll be bartender," said Danny.

"Help yourselves to nibbles too," said Mr. Jordan.

"I think I'll sign up for drama class again next year," said Ginny between bites of pizza. "All that rehearsing is worth it."

"Ginny is a pizza freak," said Beth.

"A pizza gourmet," said Ginny, pronouncing the word grr-met with a phony French accent.

"She's not a French language expert though," teased Kevin.

"Zen you must teach me, cherie," said Ginny.

"Come wiz me to zee corner," said Kevin, taking her hand.

Ginny winked at Beth and followed Kevin.

"Looks like those two are getting serious," said Matt.

"Yes. They make a nice couple," said Beth. And so do we, she thought, looking up at Matt.

"Matt, would you help me move the furniture?" asked Mr. Jordan. "I'll put some music on."

"Sure, Mr. Jordan."

Beth moved out of the way so the moving could be

done. She was standing in the hall, thinking about Matt, the play, Ginny and Kevin, when two arms slipped tightly around her waist. She jumped.

"Hi, stranger." She looked back over her shoulder. Sandy grinned at her.

She pushed his arms back and stepped away from him.

"You were OK on stage, Laurey," he said. "How about going to The Wharf with me after the play tomorrow night?"

Beth stared at him, not knowing whether to laugh or explode. Instead she smiled sweetly. "I suggest you ask Elsa," she said, staring into Sandy's dark eyes.

His smile faded. "Mind your own business," he said.

"Hey, what's going on here?" Matt put his hands on Beth's shoulders. "Beth is my girl now. She's going to dinner with me tomorrow night."

"Yeah," said Sandy. "I should have known." He turned away and pushed through the crowd.

"I am?" asked Beth, turning to look up at Matt.

"Am what?" he asked, then mussed her hair.

She shook her head. "Am your girl? Am going out to dinner tomorrow night?"

"Both, I hope." Suddenly he was the shy Matt Morrow again. "I've been meaning to ask if you'd—Will you go with me, at least until the end of the summer?"

"And what happens after that?"

"I'll be leaving for school. I'm not sure it would be fair to ask you to be my girl when I'm not here."

"Can't we decide that in August?" asked Beth.

"You mean you will? Yes? Go with me now?" He stumbled over his words.

She laughed.

He didn't look or sound like the star of *Oklahoma!*

"Yes, I'd be proud to be your girl, Matt," she said.

He took both her hands in his and stood staring down into her eyes. For a few seconds, Beth felt that she and Matt were the only two in the room.

"Hey, you two, dance or move."

Beth returned from dreamland. Matt took her in his arms. The tape that was playing was slow. "My parents wondered if you and your family would join us for dinner after the play tomorrow night."

"I'm sure they will, but I'll have to ask."

"I'll call you tonight," said Matt.

The next song was fast, Matt and Beth wandered to the side of the room.

"What did you say to Sandy about Elsa?" asked Matt.

"She's always cared a lot about him. I just thought he should notice." She looked up at Matt and smiled. "I'm so happy," she said.

"Good," said Matt. "So am I." He looked at his watch. "Are you ready to go home?"

"Yes," said Beth. "I'll find the others."

Neither Ginny and Kevin nor Danny and Joan were ready to leave. They said they'd get rides from someone else. Beth and Matt said goodbye to Mr. and Mrs. Jordan and thanked them for the party.

"You two get a lot of rest for the big day tomorrow," said Mr. Jordan. "No late night date for either of you."

"We'll be fine," said Beth. "Don't worry."

Mr. Jordan smiled. "I can't fool you kids for a minute," he said walking them to the door. "You'd think I was directing my first play."

The sun was setting; the gray-pink of evening spread across the sky. Soon the sky would be dark.

Matt opened the car door for Beth. After he slid into the driver's seat, he leaned over and kissed her. It was one day she'd remember forever.

Matt drove slowly. Before they reached Beth's house, he turned the car into the library parking lot. He turned the headlights off as he stopped the car near the hedge that separated the lot from the building, then turned to Beth. "I love you, Beth," he said.

"I love you, too," she answered as he took her into his arms. She knew that she really did love him. This time her love was real.

CHAPTER TWENTY-SIX

Oklahoma!—*Meridian High*

Matt and Beth as Curly and Laurey concluded the love song, "People Will Say We're in Love."

I wonder if the audience can tell that we really are? thought Beth.

The curtain fell, and still the audience clapped and called for more. The curtain parted. Matt and Beth stepped forward, holding hands. There were cheers.

"Thank you. You're a marvelous audience," said Matt. "But we wouldn't have had a successful play tonight without the dedication and encouragement of our drama teacher, Mr. Jordan."

Everyone clapped more.

Mr. Jordan came from the wings.

"We want to present you with this plaque to show our appreciation for all your hard work," said Beth. She held up the walnut square faced with gold metal. A tiny surrey was engraved at the bottom. The words said: IN RECOGNITION OF ROBERT JORDAN, A TEACHER WHO IS O-K.

Again everyone burst into applause as Mr. Jordan read the words. "Thank you, everyone," he said. "Parents, you have some wonderful kids."

Beth expected the curtain to close. Instead, Matt stepped forward. "I'd like to present a tribute to my leading lady, Beth Winston," he said.

Ginny ran from the wings and handed him a huge bouquet of pink roses. He put them in Beth's arms.

With tears streaming down her face, Beth tried to smile. "I kept telling him not to throw flowers at me," she said. "He simply didn't listen."

The audience cheered.

The entire cast stepped forward and bowed once more as the orchestra played the finale. The curtain closed for the last time.

"I'm going to The Wharf with Kevin," said Ginny as she came to bury her face in the roses. "Mmm. How I love flowers."

"Ginny, did you know about this?" asked Beth.

"Have to go," said Ginny, hurrying away.

Beth smiled. She looked around for Matt, but he had disappeared too.

Beth hurried to change from her costume to her blue dress. She gathered the flowers, then went to find Matt. Earlier they'd agreed they would meet by the side door of the auditorium.

"Matt, why didn't you tell me about these flowers?" she said. "I never suspected you were going to do that."

"Good. I didn't want to spoil the surprise. You certainly did find an appropriate line."

Beth looked at him. His eyes sparkled. He looked like a college student already—a man, in his gray pants, blue shirt, dark tie, and navy blazer. She felt a lump in her throat and tears threaten. "Thanks, Matt, for everything," she said.

"Thank you," he replied, putting an arm around her. "Let's go find our parents."

The Winstons and the Morrows had identified each other and were talking when Matt and Beth joined them. Beth could guess how they knew each other. Mr. Morrow was Matt a little older, a little heavier, and with some gray at the temples. Mrs. Morrow had the same beautiful, thick-lashed eyes that Beth loved so much.

Her parents hugged her and congratulated both of them.

"You must be Lisa," said Beth, noticing a young girl, who looked very much like Matt's mother, standing quietly nearby.

"Yes," she said. "I'd know you were Beth even if Matt wasn't with you. He described you perfectly."

Beth wondered what words Matt had used, but she felt too shy to ask in front of everyone.

"You were surprised by the flowers, weren't you?" said Lisa. "I knew you would be. I couldn't wait. That was the best part of the play."

Everyone laughed.

"Let's eat," said Matt. "I'm starved."

Mr. Morrow had made reservations at Gordon's Galley. The restaurant brought back memories of that other *Oklahoma!* production. Beth wondered if Matt was remembering too.

What a wonderful end to an already wonderful day, she thought as she sipped a spoonful of fresh vegetable soup and listened to her parents laugh and talk with Matt's parents. She looked up and saw Matt watching her. He winked.

* * *

How quickly the old routine seemed to return. The only difference was that Beth now worked alternate days with Ginny. She clutched her school books and hurried across to the library. It was her day.

"A marvelous production," said Mrs. Forest as Beth slid her school books under the counter.

"Thank you," said Beth. She looked to see if Matt was at his usual study table. He'd said he would meet her at the library but had to do something first. His chair was empty. Beth was disappointed.

There were only a couple of weeks left until Matt's graduation. I'll have to find a special gift for him, thought Beth as she pushed the cart forward, then looked to see which books had to be shelved next.

She moved along the nonfiction aisles, putting books about gardening, medicine, architecture, and music in their places. When she reached the theatre section, a flood of memories chased through her mind.

Beth reached down to pick up the books for this section.

Silent Movies. The title with the blurred *i* leaped out at her. Beth gasped as she saw an envelope poking from the center of the book. She pulled it out, tore it open and read:

Dear Beth,

I wanted to put these words in writing: I love you!

S. W. A. K. (Sealed With A Kiss)

Matt

Beth looked up to see Matt peeking around the

side of a shelf. He winked and pulled back.

She felt like laughing and shouting and dancing. She was loved and in love, a marvelous feeling.